"Where can we find safety?"

"The trees," Ezra said as they ran toward the thicker part of the forest, the chopper too close for comfort.

As she sprinted ahead of him, Clarissa stumbled. Ezra caught her and backed up to a tree, clutching her close.

The noise of the helicopter faded. He was aware of her palms pressed against his chest, and his heart skipped a beat.

"Do you think we lost them?"

"Wait awhile longer," he said. Her proximity made his skin tingle but he stepped back. He knew enough to know that people had let her down when she'd needed them. He wouldn't destroy the fragile trust he saw in her eyes.

"Ezra, why are you helping me?"

His commitment went beyond responsibility to a client. He felt something much deeper for her. He couldn't bring himself to say it, though. "Because you deserve better than having some murderer chase you through the woods."

And unless they got moving, that was exactly what she'd get.

Books by Sharon Dunn

Love Inspired Suspense

Dead Ringer
Night Prey
Her Guardian
Broken Trust
Zero Visibility
Guard Duty
Montana Standoff
Top Secret Identity
Wilderness Target

SHARON DUNN

has always loved writing, but didn't decide to write for publication until she was expecting her first baby. Pregnancy makes you do crazy things. Three kids, many articles and two mystery series later, she still hasn't found her sanity. Her books have won awards, including a Book of the Year Award from American Christian Fiction Writers. She was also a finalist for an *RT Book Reviews* Inspirational Book of the Year Award.

Sharon has performed in theater and church productions, has degrees in film production and history, and worked for many years as a college tutor and instructor. Despite the fact that her résumé looks as if she couldn't decide what she wanted to be when she grew up, all the education and experience have played a part in helping her write good stories.

When she isn't writing or taking her kids to activities, she reads, plays board games and contemplates organizing her closet. In addition to her three kids, Sharon lives with her husband of twenty-two years, three cats and lots of dust bunnies. You can reach Sharon through her website, www.sharondunnbooks.net.

WILDERNESS TARGET

SHARON DUNN

HARLEQUIN® LOVE INSPIRED® SUSPENSE

Recycling programs
for this product may
not exist in your area.

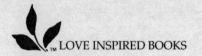

™ LOVE INSPIRED BOOKS

ISBN-13: 978-0-373-67630-9

WILDERNESS TARGET

www.Harlequin.com

Printed in U.S.A.

According as he hath chosen us in him
before the foundation of the world, that
we should be holy and without blame before him
in love: having predestinated us unto the
adoption of children by Jesus Christ to himself,
according to the good pleasure of his will.
—*Ephesians* 1:4–5

To Jonah, the bravest person I know.

ONE

Clarissa Jones quickened her pace through the tiny airport that serviced Discovery, Montana. Fear shot through her when she looked back at the barrel-chested man making a beeline for her. Why had one of her former boss's employees followed her here?

Max Fitzgerald owned one of the largest real estate and property management firms in Southern California, and the man coming after her hauled furniture for him when he staged houses. As Max's assistant—up until two weeks ago—Clarissa had known all the people Max employed. This man, whose first name was Don, had displayed a temper on more than one occasion.

Don caught up with her, grabbing her arm just above the elbow. "I think you better come with me."

She recoiled from the pressure as the man's meaty fingers dug into her flesh. Max had been angry when she'd refused his advances, and even angrier when she'd told his wife. But having his hired muscle chase her all the way to Montana seemed a bit extreme even for a hothead like Max Fitzgerald.

"Let go of me." Pain shot through her nerve endings as she tried to pull away.

Several people craned their heads in her direction. Don glanced from side to side, suddenly aware of the spectators around them, and lightened his grip on her arm.

"He wants you on a flight back to California tonight." The man spoke in a hushed tone, but the threat of violence in his eyes terrified Clarissa.

The hired muscle had been one of the last ones on the plane. She'd managed to avoid him for the whole of the flight, but now there was little chance of escape.

Clarissa squared her shoulders and looked Don in the eye. "I don't want anything to do with that man anymore."

Why was Max doing this? Was this about revenge or control? She had expected to be fired when she'd refused his advances. She'd spent ten years working her way up from the cleaning crew. She'd been his assistant for less than a month. Up until then, the veneer of her employer's charisma and her minimal contact with him had masked who he really was.

Her newfound faith had compelled her to tell Mrs. Fitzgerald what kind of man she was married to. Stella Fitzgerald had been grateful— and apparently had immediately confronted her husband. Days later, when Clarissa had told him she was going to file wrongful dismissal charges against him, Max, who had access to her personal information, had stopped direct deposit on her paycheck and used his position as owner of her apartment building to get her evicted. The final nail in the coffin of her life in California was when Max filed charges saying she'd embezzled company funds. She'd gone to the police, but by then her reputation was so smeared they didn't take her claims seriously. Max was a respected businessman, while she was homeless and jobless, with no one on her side.

So she had decided to return to Discovery after ten years away to start over. And now Max's muscle had followed her here. Where would his desire for revenge end?

Don leaned close to her, eyes bloodshot, breath hot on her face. "Now you listen to me. We're going to go down to that ticket counter and you're going to buy a one-way ticket to L.A. Max wants to talk to you."

Clarissa gasped. The threat of violence stained his every word. Fear squeezed her heart like a vise. She glanced around. She could scream right now, but somehow she thought better of it. She didn't know what this man was capable of.

A group of people swarmed toward the baggage claim as the first suitcase appeared on the carousel.

Stay with the crowd and he can't hurt you.

She pulled free of his grip and stalked toward baggage claim, but then dived into the ladies' room. He wouldn't follow her here. She hid in a stall, taking in a deep breath to ease the rising panic.

It was close to 11:00 p.m. now. An airport this small probably pretty much shut down by midnight. She listened to women chatting, water being turned on and the hand drier blowing. Forty-five minutes passed. She couldn't stay in here forever.

Was he just outside, waiting to grab her? She opened the door to the stall. A young woman with a backpack stood drying her hands.

Clarissa stepped toward her. "Can you do me a favor? Could you look and see if there's a large man in a brown sport coat standing outside? He has short, spiky hair."

The woman smiled. "Trouble with the boyfriend, huh?"

Clarissa didn't bother to correct the woman's assumption. "If you could just look, I'd be so grateful."

The woman nodded, disappeared and then came back a moment later. "You're clear."

Clutching her handbag, Clarissa raced out to the main area of the airport. Don was at the other end by a snack cart with his back to her. She assessed her options.

Four people stood in line at the rental car agency—if she tried to join the line, there would be too much risk of being noticed while she waited. She ran toward the sliding doors just as the thug turned in her direction. Clarissa breathed in clean night air as she scrambled to come up with a plan of escape. If memory served from the time she'd lived here as a teenager, the town of Discovery was eight or ten miles from the airport.

There were several hotel shuttle buses, but no taxis.

A set of doors farther down opened, and Don stepped out. Clarissa slipped into the shadows by the brick building. She held her breath, fearing that even exhaling would alert him to her presence. He lumbered down the sidewalk of the unloading zone, away from her.

A broad-shouldered man with light brown hair got out of a van that was parked in the shuttle lane. The graphic on the side said Jefferson Expeditions. He walked toward the airport holding a clipboard. He hadn't locked the doors, probably thinking whoever he was picking up would just let themselves in.

Max's thug was talking to a woman who had emerged from the airport and was facing away from her. This was Clarissa's chance to escape. She ran toward the van with the unlocked doors. This had to work. She needed to get into town. Hopefully, the van driver wouldn't be checking IDs. The vehicle could hold at least twelve people. Maybe he wouldn't even notice her. If he did, she could offer to pay. Anything to get away from Don and into town.

Within minutes, a forty-something couple crawled into the seat in front of her.

The woman adjusted her canvas hat and turned toward Clarissa. "Hi, I'm Jan and this is my husband, Kenneth."

"I'm Clarissa."

"So this survival school should be pretty unique." Jan smoothed her shirtfront. "I know Ken and I are excited. We do a lot of hiking and camping, but we haven't ever done anything like this."

Clarissa nodded in agreement.

"Have you met Ezra?" Jan pointed out the window at the man with the clipboard, who was shaking the hand of a younger man who looked as if he was barely out of high school.

As she watched Ezra help the young man with his suitcases, anxious thoughts tumbled through her head. Maybe this had been a mistake. "We're going into Discovery first, right?"

"Yes, we'll spend the night there, and in the morning we're off on our wilderness adventure." Jan furled her brow. "Didn't you get the itinerary? Ezra emailed it to everybody days ago." The woman narrowed her eyes.

Clarissa laced her fingers together, hoping her voice didn't give away the level of panic she felt. "I've been so busy at work trying to wrap things up. Guess I forgot to check my email. I had to race to the airport, and I almost missed my flight." She hated telling lies. Could she even pull this off?

Jan's expression brightened, all doubt falling away. "I understand. You can look at my itinerary if you want to refresh your memory." She dug through her bag.

"I'm sure Ezra will go through everything before he turns us loose in the woods." Kenneth broke his silence. "This guy should be pretty good. His bio on the website said he's ex-military."

More people piled into the van, a blond with a deep tan, a twenty-something couple and several others. Clarissa had chosen the middle of the middle seat, hoping that would shield her from view. The tinted windows helped, too. All the same, she slumped down to be less noticeable from the outside. Now if only Ezra wouldn't give her up.

The young man he had been talking to earlier wedged in beside Clarissa, providing even more of a shield. He held out his hand to her. "Hi, I'm Bruce Finch, from New Hampshire." Bruce was thin and light complected. If she had to guess, she'd say he worked in an office.

"My name is Clarissa." She shook his hand quickly, hoping he wouldn't notice the trembling in her fingers.

A man with glasses took the front passenger seat. He turned to introduce himself, and a moment later, most of the people in the van were engaged in a discussion about whether they were doing the two-day survival course with a man named Jack or the weeklong one with Ezra.

Clarissa closed her eyes and willed her heart to slow down. The voices around her faded. How had her life gotten to this point of desperation? She'd tried to do the right thing. She'd worked hard for ten years. As a homeless teenager, she'd been given a job on Max's cleaning crew, even though she was only fifteen. That he had been willing to hire her illegally should have been her first clue as to what kind of man Max really was. But she'd been desperate and hungry. She'd finished her GED and taken college classes at night, until she'd been promoted to the position of his assistant. The day she'd started that job, she'd thought she had put a childhood of neglect behind her.

The back hatch of the van flipped open. Ezra's warm tenor voice floated in on the night air. "Just be a minute here, folks, while I load up."

Clarissa sank down farther into the seat, not daring to turn around. Some of the seats in the van were still unoccupied. That clipboard he hauled around probably had a list of who he was supposed to pick up. Why had she ever thought this would work?

Please, God, don't let him toss me out.

The first suitcase hit the floor of the van with a thud. "So glad…everyone could make it without any flight delays."

Clarissa tensed, anxious thoughts plaguing her. She'd heard the stutter in his voice. No doubt he'd counted heads and seen that there was one too many. Her mind scrambled to come up with an excuse before he kicked her out on the curb.

The back hatch closed.

"Excuse me, sir, I'm wondering if you have

seen a woman—blond, skinny, wearing a gray suit." Clarissa's stomach coiled into a tight knot as Don's gruff voice came through an open window.

Ezra said, "Why are you looking for her?"

"I thought I saw her walking over this way. If you don't mind, I'd like to check in your van."

"Are you a police officer? Is she in trouble with the law?" Ezra's voice held unexpected resolve.

A tense silence followed.

Don lowered his voice a notch, rage evident in each syllable despite the forced courtesy of his words. "If I could just have a look inside your van…"

Clarissa dug her fingers into the armrest.

Bruce leaned toward her. "You all right?"

She managed a spastic smile. "Just tired and tense from the flight, I guess." Her heartbeat drummed in her ears.

She turned her attention back to the conversation outside the van. Ezra's answer was a long time in coming. When he did respond, he spoke deliberately. "Sir, it's clear you have no authority to search my van. These people are my paying customers. They signed up for a survival class, not to be harassed. Good day."

Ezra's footsteps pounded around the side of the van.

The tension Clarissa had felt since leaving California eased from her muscles. She was safe for now.

Ezra slipped into the driver's seat. She felt self-conscious as he peered in the rearview mirror at her. She studied the back of his head where his brown hair touched the collar of his flannel shirt. She breathed a silent prayer of thanks for Ezra. But why had he protected her?

Ezra caught a glimpse of the blonde woman with the delicate features in his rearview mirror. He'd first noticed her as she'd stepped out of the airport, clutching her bag to her chest. Everything about her, from the high heels to the gray suit that showed off her curves, said city girl. But it was the look on her face right before she'd slipped into the shadows by the building that had stabbed at his heart. He'd seen something that ran deeper than fear in her expression and body language. The woman had been terrified.

As he pulled out onto the road that led back to Discovery, he wondered what her story was. Who was she and who was the rude man who was looking for her?

He let go of his speculation about the blonde woman and tuned into the small talk of the other clients. He loved the sense of excitement they had at the prospect of a week in the woods learning survival skills. Forget the vacations where people lounged on beaches and had meals brought to them. He taught people how to find their own food, build shelters and work together. In the process, he made them feel better about themselves and what they could accomplish.

The headlights ate up the yellow line on the highway as the warm glow of a thousand lights indicated that they were nearing Discovery.

He glanced one more time at the woman in the middle seat. Was the guy back at the airport an angry boyfriend?

Ezra still wasn't sure what impulse had made him not turn her over to the gruff man with more muscles than social skills.

His experience in the wild had taught him to read the signals for when an animal would charge or run away. And something about that man gave off a dangerous vibe that seemed to say his intention was to hurt the woman. Getting her away from him had seemed the only option.

That said, Ezra had no desire to get involved with whatever trouble she'd brought with her. The slight build and soft features reminded him of his little sister. Melissa had been the only girl in a family of four boys. They'd doted on her, spoiled her, loved her. But it hadn't been enough. Neither he nor his brothers had been aware of how controlling the man she was dating was…until it was too late. Melissa had married and moved to another state, cutting off all contact with the family.

It still broke Ezra's heart. He hadn't been able to protect his little sister. Was he trying to make up for it by helping this woman? He'd like to think he could have made a difference for Melissa if he'd acted earlier—but he couldn't change that now. Helping this woman wouldn't bring his sister back. And besides, he knew nothing about her. It wasn't his place to interfere in her life or her problems.

He glanced into the rearview mirror one more time. She was scared and alone. He could at least give her a ride into town. His kindness didn't need to extend any further than that.

He slowed down as he entered the city limits. He drove past a pizza place full of late-night activity, along with offices, art galleries and boutiques. Discovery was known as the gateway to Yellowstone Park, but the town was surrounded by wilderness. People bought vacation homes here to take advantage of the skiing in winter and hiking in the summer. The core population hovered around fifty thousand.

He pulled up beside the Jefferson Expeditions office. After coming to a stop, he turned to face the people in the van. "Okay, folks, get a good night's sleep. The Black Bear Inn is just across the street. Those of you doing the weekend school, my partner, Jack, will meet up with you in the hotel lobby at 0900. The people signed up for the one-week school will meet me back here at 0800 so we can get you equipped and go over some survival basics."

The blonde woman looked away, refusing to make eye contact. Doors were pushed open, and people eased out of the van. Ezra opened the hatch and pulled out suitcases.

He handed Jan her suitcase.

"That's the last time you are going to carry our luggage for us, right?" she joked.

Ezra shook his head and laughed. "You'll have fun, trust me."

One by one, the clients headed up the sidewalk, the wheels of their suitcases bumping over the concrete. The blonde woman was not with them. When he looked around, there was no sign of her. He shrugged off a nagging sense of worry for her. He'd gotten her safely to town. She could probably take care of herself now. Besides, he'd be heading off to the wilderness in the morning—the last place a city girl like her belonged. Surely he'd done all for her that he could.

TWO

Clarissa slipped down the first alley she came to. She didn't want to involve Ezra any further in this tangled mess. Maybe it was just because she had been on her own since she was fourteen, but she'd gotten into the habit of not expecting help from anyone. She could fix this by herself. She'd find another job. She'd get a new start somewhere else.

She shifted her handbag to her shoulder and walked on. Maybe she should go to the police. *And tell them what?* she wondered. They couldn't fix what had taken place in California.

She had a natural distrust of the police from her teen years, and knowing that the police had been dismissive of her claims in California made her worry that they would do the same here. Really, she had known from the moment Max fired her that she should cut her losses rather than try to take on the legal and financial resources Max had access to. She just had no idea he would go so far as to send Don after her. It didn't make any sense. Why couldn't Max be happy with her leaving the state? Why did he want her to come back?

She stepped out onto a side street. Things looked different after ten years. But then, she supposed she was different, too. For one thing, she'd found faith in the time since she'd been gone. And that reminded her of the friend who had helped with that—a friend she hoped could help her again now.

Sondra had been a maid employed in Max's house. Because she had started out on Max's cleaning crew, Clarissa had felt a kinship to her. But Sondra had been more than a friend. She was the person who had taken the seeds of faith that had been planted in Clarissa ten years ago, when she'd been a scared, pregnant teenager here in Discovery, and helped them flower. Clarissa had witnessed love and grace at Naomi's Place, a home for pregnant teens, but it had taken a decade for the message to sink in. And it never could have happened without Sondra.

She'd been fired about the time Clarissa had gotten her promotion. Sondra had cleaned Max's office on a Tuesday, when it was supposed to be cleaned on a Wednesday. Right before she'd left, Sondra had pressed a piece of paper with her phone number and address on it into

Clarissa's hand. "If you ever need anything, give me a call."

At the time, Clarissa had wondered why Sondra's words were so filled with desperation. As someone who worked in his mansion, maybe she had known what kind of man Max really was.

Clarissa wandered through the town, trying to remember the location of things. First, she needed to find a safe, quiet place to call Sondra. The streets were nearly abandoned at this hour and most places were closed. Her heart squeezed tight as anxiety returned. Would Max's thug follow her here? He must have figured out she was in the van. It would take him a while to get a rental car or taxi. That bought her some time.

Why had she come back to Discovery anyway? She'd stood at the airport counter in LAX. The attendant had asked her where she wanted to go, his gaze heavy and demanding. She had blurted out Discovery without thinking.

Sondra lived about a day's drive away, in Wyoming. Glancing nervously up and down the alley, Clarissa pulled out her phone and searched for the crumpled piece of paper. She walked a couple more blocks until she spotted a coffee shop. She ordered a herbal tea and found a secluded booth away from the only other patrons. The posted hours said they closed in twenty minutes.

She stared at her phone. It was late. Would Sondra even pick up? Clarissa pressed the numbers and put the phone to her ear.

"Hello."

She let out a sigh of relief when she heard her friend's voice. "Sondra, it's me, Clarissa." She gripped the phone a little tighter. Asking for help had always been hard for her.

"Hey, kiddo, it's good to hear from you."

The welcoming tone in Sondra's voice made Clarissa smile. Sondra had been a true friend. Clarissa wasn't sure why Sondra called her kiddo; they were maybe ten years apart, but it made her feel cared for, as if she was someone Sondra wanted to look after.

"So what's going on?" she asked.

Clarissa closed her eyes and thought through what she would say. "I'm in some trouble. It's Max." She opted for the shorter version of what had happened. She could give Sondra the full details later. "He fired me, and I've left California. I don't have a car."

Sondra hesitated in answering. "Where are you now?"

"I'm in Discovery. I remembered where you lived, so I called." Clarissa tensed, half expecting her to say the drive would be too much trouble.

"I can be there in seven hours. I'll leave right away. Tell me where to pick you up at."

Clarissa felt a rush of gratitude. "Oh, Sondra, thank you so much." She thought about possible meeting places. "There's a bench outside the Black Bear Inn downtown. I'll be sitting on that."

"See you then," Sondra said. "And kiddo, it's good to hear your voice."

Feeling a sense of hope, Clarissa shut off her phone. Now all she had to do was find lodging for the night. She opened her handbag. In an effort to get away from Don, she'd left her checked baggage at the airport, but at least she still had her wallet. In it was enough cash to pay for a hotel room.

She finished her tea and left the coffee shop. She turned the corner, back toward the Black Bear Inn. As Ezra's van had come into town, she hadn't noticed any other hotel within walking distance. If she hurried, she could get checked in before Max's thug showed up. Far better than wandering the streets trying to find a different hotel. Staying outside would only make her vulnerable. Though it was several blocks away, she could see that the lights in Ezra's office were still on. The memory of what he had done for her brought some guilt to the surface. She really did need to thank him for his kindness.

Ezra pulled some food and other supplies from a cupboard in a back room, then worked his way around stacks of boxes in the hallway. The office was more of a storage space for backpacks, tents and other supplies than it was an office. Surrounded by packets of dried food, his computer was barely visible on the desk.

"My conscience wouldn't let me leave without saying thank you. The light was on, so I..."

Ezra whirled around to face the petite blonde woman. She must have come in when he was in the back room. Her voice had a soft, hypnotic quality, like wind rushing through trees.

He placed the boxes of supplies on the desk. "Yeah, sure, no problem." A war raged within him. He still had a lot of prep to do before morning, and the last thing he needed was a woman bringing trouble with her. At the same time, when he looked at this woman, he wondered if he could have done something different so Melissa would still be in his life. He couldn't undo what had happened with his sister. His conscience would be clear if he knew he'd done everything he could for this woman.

She pressed the large handbag she'd brought

with her closer to her body. "I wanted to thank you for your kindness, is all."

She stood before him, the blouse and tailored jacket a little disheveled. Her blue eyes held a pleading quality.

"What is your name?"

Her expression softened. "Clarissa."

He stepped toward her. "Listen, Clarissa, I don't know what is going on with you and that guy who was looking for you. I can take you up to the police station if that would help." He pointed in that general direction.

"No…" She took a step back and a wall seemed to go up around her. Panic coated her words. "I'll be all right. I'm…I'm meeting someone tomorrow."

Again, he wondered what she was afraid of, and why the man was after her. That she didn't want to go to the police made him a little suspicious. Maybe she wasn't the fragile innocent she projected. "Are you sure? I know some of the local guys. I'm positive they'd help you out… whatever the trouble is."

"This isn't a police matter." She seemed to grow more upset with each word. Shaking her head, she took another step back. "Please, I just wanted to thank you for getting me into town." She turned and pulled the door open. He heard her hurried footsteps on the sidewalk as the door eased shut.

He had offered help, and she had refused. There was nothing more he could do. He had to let it go.

Clarissa made her way up the street. A cluster of people spilled out of a steak house. Laughing and talking, they skirted around her on the sidewalk. She glanced back, half hoping to see Ezra. His concern had been so unexpected, she found herself drawn to him. The lights in his office clicked off, but he didn't come out. There must be a back door to the office, likely one that led to a parking area with his personal car.

She made her way across the street. The lobby of the Black Bear Inn was still illuminated. She'd used up precious time in saying thank-you to Ezra—time Don could have used to reach Discovery—but her conscience wouldn't allow her to leave town without letting him know that he had done the right thing by sticking his neck out for her.

A rental car eased down the street, as though the driver was looking for something.

Clarissa's breath hitched, and she took a step back. Blood whooshed in her ears.

Max's hired muscle got out of the rental car,

his narrow-eyed gaze slicing through her. He slammed the door and bolted toward her.

She kicked off her high heels. Adrenaline charged through her as she ran barefoot up the side street. The people from the steak house had gotten in their cars and driven away. No one else was around. When she ran past the coffee shop, it was dark. Maybe she could double back and slip into the safety of the steak house.

She willed her feet to pump harder, not daring to look over her shoulder. She ran past a library with darkened windows, and into a park. With her heart pounding, Clarissa made her way toward the playground equipment. She charged up the stairs of the slide and slipped into the tiny enclosure at the top, pressing her knees against her chest. Breathless from her run, she struggled to stay silent.

She closed her eyes and waited, listening. Had she shaken him off? Gradually, her breathing slowed to normal. She leaned back against the hard metal of the enclosure. She relaxed a little.

And then she heard it—the crunch of a footstep on the wood chips that surrounded the playground equipment.

Clarissa froze, holding her breath. She could hear him moving around the area. His footsteps faded and then grew louder. She recognized the distinctive sound of a foot touching metal. He was coming up the steps. She swung around and pushed off down the slide. Her feet hit the ground, and she took off across the rolling hills of the park, back toward downtown. She could hear him now, his footsteps rapid and closing in.

She ran harder. Rocks bruised her bare feet.

Don grabbed her arm and yanked her back. She swung around, hitting his face with her purse. He grunted and let go. She turned to run, getting only a few steps before she felt the weight of his hands on her shoulders, taking her down. Her stomach impacted with the ground, knocking the wind out of her. She pushed up on all fours and tried to crawl away, but he grabbed her foot. Clarissa flailed, trying to kick free.

"Quit it," he growled.

She kicked his arm. She wasn't giving up without a fight. He moaned from the pain, grabbed hold of her wrists and jerked her up. She twisted from side to side, seeking to break free.

"Stop it, I said." His breath smelled of cigarettes.

She stilled, catching her breath and trying to come up with her next move. She had to get away from this man. "I'm not going back to California."

Don chuckled. "No, you're not." His voice was sinister. "You know what Max liked about you? That you had no family. No one to notice or care that you were gone."

He let go of her wrists. She crab-walked backward. He lunged at her, wrapping his hands around her neck. Fear shot through her. She scratched and pulled at his wrists, but he pressed harder. She struggled for air as she clawed at his forearms and then tried to pry his fingers off. She saw spots before her eyes. The air left her lungs.

Up the hill, headlights cut a swath of illumination across the park. The car came to a stop and laughing teenage voices filled the still night air.

The thug loosened his grip on Clarissa's neck. She gasped for air. The teenagers were headed toward them. One of them shouted, "Hey, what's going on there?"

Don let go of her neck altogether. She flipped over and took off running. She could hear the thug talking to the teens, telling lies, no doubt. She headed down the hill toward the library. It was closed, but the building might offer a nook or cranny where she could hide.

Max's henchman wasn't going to give up, but he wouldn't try anything as long as she was within screaming range of the teenagers. She'd never in her life been so glad for teenagers ignoring park curfew rules.

She slipped into a dark alcove in the library exterior wall, pressing hard against it. He wouldn't see her here. Moments later, she heard his footsteps on the concrete walk. The noise faded slowly. Her fingers touched her neck. Warm tears formed.

She squeezed her eyes shut. She wouldn't give in to crying. She was a fighter, a survivor. She would get out of this alive. Clarissa squared her shoulders and lifted her chin. She waited at least ten more minutes before stepping out of the shadows and walking toward the lights of downtown.

She stayed alert, looking from side to side and listening for footsteps. Of course, Don would return to the street where he'd parked. Still, the Black Bear Inn seemed like her best option. Staying on the street looking for a hotel only increased the odds of him finding her again. Somehow she'd managed to hold on to her purse, all she had in the world. She could afford to get a room for the night.

She walked one block past Main Street and then circled back to the inn until she found a side door. Pausing outside, she straightened her clothes, buttoned her blazer and ran her fingers through her hair.

The lobby held a warm glow. She walked toward the check-in desk, where a college-aged man hunched over a notebook computer. If she looked out of sorts, he gave no hint of it in his expression, and he didn't stare at her bare feet. She appreciated his professional demeanor.

"Can I get a room, please?"

"We have one single left," he said.

"That would be fine."

He pulled a key off the wall and slid it across the counter before shifting over to the hotel computer. "It's eighty dollars a night. How will you be paying?"

"Cash." Clarissa opened her purse and stared down at the pile of bills. The day she'd left California, she'd gone back to Max's house to plead with him to drop the charges and give her the money she was owed. He had not been home, but his wife had been. When Stella Fitzgerald found out how Max had ruined Clarissa financially, she'd given her some money from their personal safe. Clarissa pulled out four twenties and handed them to the clerk.

"Have a good night." He offered her a bolstering smile. "Your room is on the second floor at the back."

Before she left the lobby, she peered out the window that faced Main Street. Don's car was still parked across the street by the Jefferson Expeditions office. She shuddered and backed away.

She turned to face the clerk. "This place is fairly secure, isn't it?" The vibration in her voice gave away her fear.

He studied her a moment. "Sure, there'll be someone at the front desk all night. I'll be locking the side doors in ten or fifteen minutes." His voice was filled with compassion.

She hurried down the hall and up the stairs. Her hand was still shaking when she stuck the key in the hole. After locking and bolting the door, locking the windows and pulling the shades, Clarissa collapsed on the bed.

Now you can cry.

She stared at the ceiling while the warm tears flowed down her face. How had her life gotten to this point? The words of her would-be murderer came back to her. She had no family. No one to come looking for her if she went missing. She'd never known her mother, and her father had died of acute alcoholism when she was five. There had been a shining moment when she was fifteen. She'd met a boy who said he loved her, and she had believed him. She'd thought she'd never have to be alone again. Once she became pregnant, though, he had disappeared. In the end, she had miscarried, the pain of that loss almost unbearable. After that, her heart had closed off and she'd thrown herself into working hard, knowing that the only person she could depend on was herself.

Sleep came slowly, but every rattling of the window or noise in the hallway woke her. All she had to do was make it through this night. Sondra would be here in the morning. If Don was still across the street, she'd call her friend and change the pickup point. Chances were, with daylight and the streets filled with people, he wouldn't try anything. It would be best, though, that he not see her get into Sondra's car.

In the darkness of the room, Clarissa placed her hand over her throat. Don's beefy hands had almost robbed her of her last breath.

Back at the airport, Don had originally said that he wanted to take her back to California… to *talk* to Max. Thinking about it now, Clarissa decided that that had probably been a lie. Whether it happened in California or here, Max's intention had been to have her killed.

THREE

Ezra pulled the Jefferson Expeditions van up to the curb by his office. He'd taken it out early in the morning to get it gassed up and pick up some final supplies. An older man with salt-and-pepper hair stood outside the door.

Ezra shut the van door and called over to him, "Can I help you?"

"My name is Leonard Stillman, and if it's not too late, I'd like to sign up for your survival school that's headed out this morning."

Another client would really help his bottom line. It seemed a little odd, though, that the man was showing up at the last minute. "Where did you hear about Jefferson Expeditions?"

"Saw the flyer at the bait shop. I came out here for some fall fishing, but I think this survival school would be much more my speed. I like a challenge," said Leonard.

"Sure, go on inside." Ezra moved toward the door and pulled out his keys to unlock it. "Have a seat and we'll get the paperwork done. I need to get a few things out of the back of the van, but then I'll be right with you."

Leonard went inside, and Ezra opened the hatch to grab the length of rope and water filters he'd picked up at the store. He glanced across the street at the Black Bear Inn. In a little less than an hour, Jan, Ken and Bruce would be joining Leonard for a life-changing adventure.

Clarissa came out of the inn just then, glanced around and settled on a bench. Ezra waved at her, and she waved back. He went into his office, shaking his head and wondering why she looked so nervous.

Clarissa checked her watch for the third time in ten minutes. Sondra was late, and she wasn't answering her phone. Clarissa tried to free herself of the awful sinking feeling that invaded her mind.

Sondra wasn't going to show. She shouldn't have depended on her. Clarissa jumped up from the bench and paced back and forth.

If Sondra didn't show, she'd have to come up with a new plan to escape from Max. Though she hadn't seen him yet today, she was sure Don was still lurking around somewhere, waiting to catch her. She sat back down on the bench, twisting the straps of her purse.

Sondra had been a friend. Clarissa couldn't have read the signals wrong. She'd picked up on the concern in her voice when they'd spoken on the phone. Sondra wouldn't let her down.

She leaned against the wall of the Black Bear Inn and stared at her phone. There were probably places in Wyoming with no cell phone service. Maybe Sondra had been delayed, but couldn't call.

Clarissa checked her watch again. She'd wait twenty more minutes. She couldn't stay out here much longer, where Max's thug could easily spot her. A car rolled by slowly and pulled to the curb half a block away. Clarissa rose to her feet, expecting to see Sondra. Disappointment raged through her when an older man using a cane stepped to the curb.

Gazing across the street, she watched through the window of Ezra's office as he picked up backpacks and sorted through a pile of items she couldn't make out from this distance. An older man sat in a chair across from him, reading a piece of paper.

She slumped down on the bench again, clutching her purse to her chest. She had to come up with a new plan. Max's hired muscle had tried to kill her last night. That was something she could report. She would swallow her distrust of law enforcement. Ezra had pointed up the street when he'd suggested she go to the police. She walked quite a while before the station came into view, a two-story brick structure with parking lots on three sides.

She took a breath and went over in her head what she would tell them as she made her way toward the steps. But when the door of the station swung open and a man stepped out, the sight of him made Clarissa's breath hitch. She ducked behind a car. Max stood on the steps, shaking hands with a man dressed in a suit.

As she pressed herself against the back of the car, she pushed down the terror that threatened to paralyze her. That man was probably the police chief or some other law enforcement official.

Shielding herself from view by darting from car to car, Clarissa ran through the possibilities of what she could do. Max was here. And he clearly had fooled the police here just as he had in California. Any hopes that the law would actually listen to her disappeared. There was no one she could trust. She had to get out of this town and fast.

She needed time to figure out why Max wanted her dead, or she'd never be safe again. As she raced up the street, she realized she needed to hide somewhere Max would never find her, until she could work through all that had happened.

* * *

Ezra ran through a last-minute checklist of everything he needed for the survival school. He'd taken the van around to the back entrance. When he opened the door, Jan and Kenneth had already arrived to start loading their packs.

Ezra sat down at his desk and thumbed through the waivers he'd collected. With the addition of Leonard, he had four clients. Six would allow him to do more than pay the bills, but four—along with the clients Jack would be taking out—was enough to keep Jefferson Expeditions going until the next school.

The front door opened and Clarissa, his stowaway from last night, stepped in. "I'd like to go on your survival school," she stated. He thought he detected fear in her voice.

She'd changed out of the gray suit and high heels she'd been wearing into a pair of jeans, hiking boots, a light blue button-down shirt and fleece jacket. The outfit looked as if she'd just pulled it off a store rack, and yet it showed off her curves almost as nicely as the suit had.

"Your friend didn't show up, huh?"

She glanced toward the door as though she was expecting someone to burst through it. "Please, how much does the school cost? I can pay cash."

Ezra thought for a moment. Another client

would be nice, but he wasn't so sure it should be Clarissa. Trouble seemed to be following her, and his survival class was challenging enough without exposing his clients to additional danger. And just what was she mixed up in anyway? She didn't seem like the criminal type. In fact, there was an almost fragile china-doll quality to her. Maybe it was just her delicate features. He'd been deceived before by appearances.

When he'd done his tour of duty in Iraq, he had thought his fiancée, Emma, would be faithful to him. But she'd broken his heart when she'd made the excuse that she could never be married to a man who ran a wilderness survival school. Nothing was ever what it appeared to be on the surface.

Ezra straightened a pile of papers. "This is kind of last-minute." He was torn between saying yes to her and turning her away.

The back door burst open, and Jan stepped inside. "Oh, Clarissa, so good to see you. I like your outfit."

"Thanks, I just bought it this morning." Clarissa cut a sideways glance toward Ezra.

Jan turned to face him. "It's so nice to have another woman on the expedition."

A smile brightened Clarissa's face. "Yes, I'm

sure it would be hard to be the only female." She raised an eyebrow toward Ezra.

She had a point. Jan would be far less likely to give up and want to go home if she wasn't the only woman. And if Jan asked for a refund, then Kenneth probably would, too.

"So are you all ready to go?" asked Jan.

Clarissa turned back toward Ezra, amusement coloring her voice as she said, "I was just settling my bill with Mr. Jefferson, wasn't I?"

It was nice to see a playful side to her. She'd seemed so burdened by worry when he'd first met her. Whatever it was, the load she carried must be a heavy one. Would it weigh down their group? He couldn't be sure.

Ezra sighed and shook his head. "Yes, she was just getting everything in order." He hoped he wasn't making a mistake.

Jan patted her shoulder. "Good. We'll see you two in a minute. Everyone else is loaded into the van." She pulled open the back door and disappeared.

Clarissa turned to face him, her blue eyes shining. "How much do I owe you?"

Ezra placed a hand on his hip. "Are we agreed that was a little manipulative?"

"You weren't totally set on saying no to me." Her voice had a coy quality.

"That's true," he said. "The cost is twelve

hundred dollars. That includes all your supplies and a stay at a remote lodge. I'll understand if you don't have that kind of cash."

She didn't blink at the price. "No, I can pay it." She opened her purse and pulled out a stack of bills.

He tensed as suspicions rose to the surface again. Why would she have that much cash on her? He grabbed her hand. "Promise me one thing. I can't take you on this expedition if you are in trouble with the law."

She looked him in the eyes. "You don't need to hear my whole long, pathetic story. Just know that I'm not a criminal."

The steadiness of her voice and her unwavering gaze told him she was telling the truth. "Good. Let's get you geared up."

Ten minutes later, she slipped into the front passenger seat of the van. After locking up the office, Ezra got behind the wheel. He turned toward the back. "I assume everyone has been introduced." Bruce, Jan and Kenneth nodded. "Clarissa, probably the only person you don't know is Leonard. He signed up a few hours before you."

Clarissa turned to shake the hand of the fifty-ish man with the salt-and-pepper hair and deep tan.

"Well, people, the next seven days will be

brutal. You'll learn how to survive in the wilderness, how and where to find food and make a shelter. But you won't be doing it alone. One of the keys to survival is learning how to work with others. Okay, we've got a long drive up to the trailhead. This is your last chance to jump ship."

Ezra looked into the eyes of each of his clients. From his interactions with them, he'd begun to assess their strengths and weaknesses. Bruce knew more about survival in theory than in practice. Though in good shape for a man his age, Leonard could be a little overbearing, not a team player. It would be good to see Jan and Ken learn to rely on the other team members instead of just each other. Hopefully, the bond Jan had seemed to form with Clarissa would help with that.

Ezra turned to face the windshield, after glancing briefly at Clarissa. She was a mystery. He wasn't sure how she'd fit in. She struck him as a pampered city girl, but there was an inner strength there, as well. She'd piqued his curiosity. He had a feeling he wouldn't mind hearing the long pathetic story of why she needed to go on this expedition. He wouldn't mind getting to know a little more about Clarissa Jones. He only hoped that what he found out wouldn't be disastrous for this expedition.

* * *

With each mile they got farther out of town, Clarissa relaxed a little more. She checked the back window several times. No one had followed them up the winding mountain road. She pulled out her phone.

"Cell service out here is spotty at best," Ezra said.

"I'm just checking some things on my calendar." She hoped by reviewing what she and Max had worked on before he'd fired her, she might be able to figure out why he wanted her dead.

"Actually, I should have confiscated that back at the office. Everyone is required to go low-tech."

Clarissa drew her phone protectively to her chest.

Ezra chuckled at her response. "You'll only miss it for the first couple of days. After that, your hands will stop shaking from withdrawal."

Leonard leaned forward in the seat and spoke in her ear. "Actually, I think it's going to be kind of nice to get away from all that. Start looking at people's faces instead of screens."

"I think I'm going to like the quiet," said Ken.

"What if there's an emergency?" Jan asked.

"I do have a satellite phone if for any reason I need to get help to us quickly. I've never had to use it," Ezra assured them.

"I promise to leave the phone in the van." Clarissa checked her calendar itinerary quickly. Nothing stood out. "So no electronics." What else would she be giving up? She'd been so focused on finding a hiding place from Max, she hadn't really thought about what she'd signed up for.

"You can handle that, right?" Ezra tightened his grip on the wheel as the road grew steeper and more treacherous but his eyes met hers for a second.

His eyes had a bright, dancing quality that she hadn't noticed before. If leaving town made her feel safer, it seemed to make him more cheerful.

The van wound down a mountain and came out at a lake. Ezra brought the van to a stop. "This is Bridger Lake, folks—our starting point. Everyone grab your pack, double-check what you have against the inventory sheet. I always bring a few extra supplies. Limit yourself to three personal items. Leave everything else in the van. It'll be locked up. I've never had a problem with theft. My partner will come up here to check on it while we're gone."

"Three personal items," said Bruce. "It's like that riddle about being stranded on a desert island. You know, what would you take with you?"

Clarissa pushed open the door. At the back

of the van, Ezra handed her a backpack. "You missed going over what's in here. I grabbed a prepacked one for you. I'll get you up to speed when we have a moment."

She was struck by the kindness she saw in his eyes. "Thanks." Clarissa put her pack down a little distance from the others, who chattered idly with each other. They all seemed to have bonded already. She felt like the outsider. With her background, that was nothing new.

She opened her purse. She'd be hard-pressed to come up with three items that mattered to her. She removed a brown food package and a space blanket, and tucked the money at the bottom of one of the smaller compartments. Then she put the change of undergarments and shirt she'd bought in the pack, as well.

She had a picture of herself with two friends from Naomi's Place. The ten-year-old photo was worn and creased. Even though the pain of her miscarriage had caused her to run from there, the memory of the friendship she'd had with two other girls, Rochelle and Sarah, still warmed her heart. She placed the photo in one of the smaller compartments on the backpack. All her worldly treasures.

She watched Ezra, kneeling close to the van, place a small Bible in his pack. So he was a kindred spirit in that way. His faith probably ran much deeper than hers. Hers was so brand-new, and now doubt over the situation she was in had poked holes in it. She'd done the right thing by refusing Max's advances and telling his wife, and she'd lost everything because of it. She hadn't even had time to grab the Bible Sondra had given her. Uneasiness about Sondra's no-show still plagued her. What if she'd been in a car accident?

Ezra swung his backpack on. "All right, people, suit up. We leave in three minutes."

Clarissa grabbed the toothbrush and other toiletries she'd purchased that morning and packed them away. She lifted the backpack, surprised by the weight. She slipped one arm through a strap, but struggled with the other.

"Here, let me help you with that." Ezra lifted her pack from the bottom so she could slip her arm in without having to wrestle with the weight.

"Thanks."

He leaned toward her and pointed. "Belly strap."

"Oh, right." She turned slightly, looking for the other end.

He grabbed both strap ends and snapped them together. She felt the pressure of his fingers against her stomach as she met his gaze.

"You've never been on a hike before in your

life, have you?" His voice held a note of humor, not condemnation.

She shook her head. A laugh escaped her lips. "No, sorry."

He cupped his hand on her shoulder, the warmth of his touch seeping through her skin. "It's not a problem. People surprise me all the time."

She could feel her face heat up when his gaze rested on her. "I hope I can surprise you." The stir of attraction caught her off guard. She hadn't felt anything like that since she was a teenager. Back when she had been naive and had believed in fantasies like true love.

He stepped away and raised his voice. "Okay, people, single file. Let's get moving up that mountain."

Clarissa took in the beauty of the forest. The lake was like glass bordered by mountains on three sides. On the highest peak stood a fire tower surrounded by blackened trees.

Bruce came up beside her. "Guess there was a forest fire here about a month ago."

Ezra, some twenty feet away, shouted, "Visiting time is over, people. Let's get moving. Just follow the trail."

"I can't wait to get started." Bruce fell in line behind Leonard. The bow he'd strapped to his pack must have been one of his personal items.

Clarissa stepped behind Bruce. Ezra waited until they were all on the narrow trail before slipping in line behind her. As she made her way up the steep incline, she could think of a thousand reasons not to acknowledge the blossoming attraction she felt toward him. Men couldn't be trusted. Men couldn't be depended on. They left when things got difficult.

None of that reasoning did anything to stop the fluttering in her stomach every time she thought about the way he'd looked at her. How his touch brought alive emotions that she'd stuffed down for ten years.

They hiked for what felt like several hours before reaching the ridgeline. Clarissa stopped for a moment to catch her breath and examine how far they'd come. Her gaze traveled the length of the trail down to the lake where the van was.

Her breath caught as another car pulled in beside the van and two burly-looking men got out. Even from this distance, she could see that one of them was Don.

FOUR

Ezra heard the cascading rocks rolling down the steep slope before he saw them. On instinct, he grabbed Clarissa and pulled her to safety. His hand still cupped her narrow waist as half a dozen large stones rolled past them.

She touched her palm to her chest. "Way to think fast. I didn't see those coming."

"You could have been knocked over or injured." Ezra glared up the cliff to where Bruce was using his hands and feet to scale the rocky incline. "Remind me to talk to Bruce about having greater awareness of the people below him."

"You might also want to tell him that this isn't a race." Clarissa wiped the perspiration from her brow.

Ezra had to hand it to her. She'd showed substantial stamina hiking through the heat of the day. She'd kept up with the pace he'd set. Down below, Ken, Jan and Leonard made their way up the mountain. "Let's let him get farther ahead before following him—it'll be safer."

With her eyes on Bruce, Clarissa nodded in agreement.

Bruce had pushed hard all day, determined to stay in the lead, and taking very little time to notice the people around him. And Ezra had thought Leonard was going to be the lone wolf.

Clarissa stood close to him while they waited for the others to catch up. She'd pulled her silky blond hair into some sort of hair contraption. Her cheeks were flushed from the exertion of the hike.

Her gaze darted from the three stragglers to a far-off point down the trail. She'd been looking over her shoulder for most of the hike. Though she joked a great deal, every once in a while Ezra saw a flash of fear mar her features. He wondered what the cause of the jitteriness was.

"That guy at the airport, whoever he was, isn't likely to find you here." He hoped to re-assure her.

Her blue eyes locked on to him. "What makes you say that?" She turned and started on up the mountain.

The others were closing in on them. Ezra followed behind Clarissa. "I noticed you look-ing down the trail a lot. Honestly, where we're headed there's not going to be another person for fifty miles in any direction."

She stuttered in her steps, but then pushed herself onward, not looking back at him when she spoke. "There are no little towns or anything?"

"A few, way over on the other side of that mountain." He pointed off in the distance. "But we won't be going anywhere near there."

"So nothing until we get to that lodge?"

"There won't be people at the lodge, either. You can only get to it by hiking or helicopter. It's a wealthy man's rustic retreat. He lets Jefferson Expeditions use it when he's not there, for a minimal fee." Ezra caught up with her. "The only other people we might run into would be other backpackers. Does that sound okay to you?"

They both stopped climbing for a moment. Clarissa didn't completely meet his gaze, as though something still preoccupied her. "The solitude will be nice."

Jan caught up with them at last. "What a beautiful day, huh?" she said as she looked around.

The conversation drifted in another direction when Ken and Leonard joined them. As he answered their questions and got to know them better, Ezra found himself wondering what was up with Clarissa. Her questions hinted at some unspoken agenda, some plan she was making. It made him suspicious. Why, exactly, did she want to be escorted into the deep woods? He doubted he would get a straight answer from her if he asked. She was a woman with secrets and layers of protection around her.

They stopped in the late afternoon in an open area. While they ate their prepackaged snack and drank water, Ezra went over some basic rules about finding edible plants. He held up the edible plants book. "You all should have one of these in your pack. Your assignment is to spread out and come back in half an hour with something we can add to tonight's oh so appetizing MRE—Meal Ready to Eat, just like in the army. One thing to keep in mind—stay with a partner and talk loud. This is September. The bears are out filling up on food before they hibernate."

Jan let out a gasp. "Bears? This is the real thing, isn't it?"

"Absolutely," Ezra agreed. "But they're not really any more interested in running into you than you are in running into them. If you make noise, they'll most likely clear out of your way."

Clarissa unzipped a compartment of her pack and peered inside.

"Let's go over what you have in your backpack." Ezra ambled toward her.

The rest of the group scattered off, their books in hand.

"Shouldn't I be looking for plants with the others?" She continued to search the compartments, presumably looking for her book.

"The others already had this instruction from the emails I sent out, and they packed their own gear, so they know where everything is. I helped Leonard with it this morning in the office. I think it's good to have an understanding of what you have to work with, so if an emergency does come up, you can find what you need quickly." He knelt in front of her.

"I guess that makes sense." She hooked a strand of hair behind her ear and then glanced around nervously. "Guess I'm a little worried about those bears."

"I say that as a precaution. The kind of bears that are around here like to avoid people. The forest is way more safe than any big city."

She unzipped the largest compartment of her pack, pulling the supplies out, laying them on the ground. "What makes you think I'm from the city?"

He let out a huff of air. "You kind of put out that vibe that first night I met you."

"I have been living in California, but I'll have you know that I grew up in Montana. Lived in a bunch of little towns, and even in Discovery for a while." Her voice took on a faraway quality, as though there were a wealth of memories behind what she had told him.

She was full of surprises. He'd had her pegged as urban to the core. "But in all that time you never went backpacking with friends or family?"

"No, no family to go backpacking with." A shadow seemed to fall over her face, and she looked off into the distance. She regained her composure almost as quickly as she'd lost it, lifting her chin and meeting his gaze. "How about you? Did you grow up around here?"

She had a way of revealing only a small amount about herself and then deflecting the attention back on him. "Yeah, my brothers and I hunted and fished these mountains from the time we could walk."

She scooted several of the items toward him. "Why don't you tell me what all this stuff is?"

Ezra picked up the multitool and showed her what each part of it could do. "This is how you open the pliers." He wondered what had been running through her mind in that moment. How could such a benign question about hiking tap into such deep hurt?

She took the tool from him and folded out another component. "This looks like a nail file. Do you mean to tell me I'll have time for a manicure while I'm tromping around with the bears?"

He laughed, appreciating the joke, but realizing that she also used humor to divert him from thinking about her. He must have been staring a little too intensely. "The file is handy. Sometimes dirt from digging or blood from skinning an animal gets under your nails."

She made a face and jerked her head back, the usual reaction to the idea of skinning an animal.

"And sometimes you just need to file something down," said Ezra. "Let's go through the rest of the gear. Most of it is pretty straightforward."

She held up the water filter. "I don't know what this is."

"You have a day's supply of water in your pack. Beyond that, it'll be up to you to find clean water sources or use that filter to purify your water. The stuff you get from the rivers and creeks will have to be cleaned up to drink." As he instructed her about each item in the pack, he watched the sunlight play on her hair. The way she closed her eyes when she laughed was endearing. He found himself enjoying her company despite how guarded she was.

Bruce came bounding through the trees holding something in his hand. His bow was flung over his shoulder. Why he thought he needed to carry it around to look for plants, Ezra could only guess. Bruce had assured him that he knew how to use such a deadly weapon. Ezra only hoped the younger man was telling the truth.

Bruce dropped a handful of yellow flowers on the ground. "Is this evening primrose?"

Ezra picked up one of the plants. "Yes, it is. You missed out on some good eating by just picking the flower though. The roots are edible, too. They taste like parsnips."

"I'll go look for some more." He seemed encouraged by his find and tromped back toward the trees.

"Why don't I get a bow and arrow like he has?" Clarissa asked.

"That's a personal item he chose to bring. But it's not really necessary. You have things in your pack that you can use to defend yourself and even hunt with."

Clarissa examined everything that was spread out around her. She picked up a long knife in a sheath. "This, right?"

Ezra nodded, then rose to his feet. "Now I want you to put everything away, arrange things to suit yourself, so if you need to grab something in a hurry you're not fumbling in your pack."

She put the items away, so quickly that he wondered if she was even taking note of where things were going. Then she stood. "Can I go look for plants now?"

"Sure. You'll want to take the book with you and find one of the others to partner up with."

"Oh!" Clarissa laughed at herself and then leaned down and pulled the book out of a side pocket.

He watched her walk gracefully into the forest.

Clarissa quickened her pace as she moved deeper into the trees. She walked until she could no longer hear the chatter of the others as they foraged for plants. She pressed her back against an expansive evergreen and gazed up at the green canopy above her as she took a moment to regroup.

Though she had seen no sign of Max's men on the hike, her heart had been racing from the moment the car had pulled in beside the Jefferson Expeditions van. Somehow they had tracked her down. Ezra had mentioned something about a business partner. Maybe the thugs had finagled information out of him.

Don knew she'd ridden into town in Ezra's van. When they couldn't find her, they might have drawn their own conclusions, or they might have seen her going into Ezra's office. She didn't know how she'd been found; she only knew that even this forest wouldn't provide safety for her for long.

She could only hope that she might be able to keep a little ahead of the thugs. Don was muscular, but hardly the hiking type. The two men were probably not moving very fast. Maybe they wouldn't even bother following her, and would just wait to grab her until the group returned to the van.

Clarissa closed her eyes, attempting to stave off the panic that invaded her mind and body. She needed to get away and hide, but she couldn't go back the way she'd come. She'd have to get a clearer sense of where this town was that Ezra had mentioned, and then take off on her own. The people in the group seemed really likable. She didn't want them hurt at her expense. The problem was if she took off now, she might not last a day. She needed to learn everything she could from Ezra as quickly as possible.

She let out a breath. Ezra seemed like a nice man. A nice man from a nice family who went on camping trips together. His question about her not ever hiking or camping with family despite a childhood in Montana drove home a point that she'd wrestled with all her adult life. She could dress up in her business suits, get a college degree and play the competent professional. But inside, she was always the orphan set adrift in the world, tied to nobody.

She heard the sound of someone walking through the forest. Fearing that Don and his partner had already caught up with her, she slipped behind a tree. She peered around the trunk and saw Leonard standing about twenty feet from her. She opened her mouth to say hello, but stopped and slipped back out of sight when he pulled a gun from his waistband, checked it and put it back.

Her breath hitched. Fear skittered across her nerves. She watched as Leonard took out a phone, looked at it and then wandered several feet away from her. He continued to walk and check the phone, as though he was trying to get a signal.

As Leonard's footsteps faded, a hundred fear-drenched thoughts tumbled through her head. Maybe there was a sinister reason why Leonard had a gun and was trying to phone someone. He had signed up only hours before she did. Maybe Max was covering his bases and sending Leonard to kill her as soon as he got the opportunity.

"It's kind of confusing, isn't it?"

Clarissa whirled around. Jan stood a few feet away from her.

"What?"

The older woman pointed toward the book

Clarissa gripped in her hand. "Finding your next meal in the forest."

Clarissa flipped the book, looking at the back and front covers. Her hands were shaking. She still hadn't recovered from seeing Leonard with a gun. "Yeah, right, some of the poisonous ones look just like the ones you can eat."

"I'll give you a hand if you like. Ken has gone and wandered off again. We can work on it together." Jan's eyes held sincerity and warmth.

"Together?" The word felt foreign on her tongue. "I'd like that."

Jan opened her book. "I'm looking for this one." She pointed to a picture. "It says it still flowers as late as September. If you find a plant that looks like it might be edible, we can go through our books and see if we can find a match."

"That sounds like a plan," Clarissa said.

Jan gave her a friendly pat on the back. "Good."

They worked through the late afternoon, getting some assistance from Ken and showing Ezra what they'd found from time to time. Then the group hiked for several more hours before stopping to make camp. Once the camp was set up, Ezra showed Leonard how to build a fire, while Bruce practiced shooting his bow.

Clarissa watched Bruce with his bow. He hit the tree about 50 percent of the time.

"So are these brown packets our dinners?" Ken held up his. "I've never had an MRE before." He read the label. "Looks like I get chicken parmesan."

"Just add water." Leonard ripped his open. "We used to eat these all the time in the service."

Clarissa kept her eye on Leonard. She couldn't be certain he was working for Max, but she couldn't trust him, either. She just had to make sure she was never alone with him.

Jan stared down into her open bag. "This doesn't look like spaghetti and meatballs."

"Just think, tomorrow you'll be eating fresh fish or small game if you play your cards right," Ezra said.

The soft tenor of his voice drew Clarissa back to the circle of people. Bruce had come to sit in front of the fire, as well. She was going to have a hard time asking Ezra the questions she needed answers to with everyone else around.

"You mean if we catch it ourselves, we'll be eating something besides dehydrated food?" Ken said.

"That's why I bring the MREs. It motivates you to catch something fresher." Ezra's voice had a playful lilt to it.

The men and Jan groaned in unison.

"At least we got these roots and berries to help wash down the packaged food tonight." Jan picked up one of the roots and bit into it.

"How about you, Clarissa?" Ezra turned to face her. "I don't hear much protest from you."

With everyone looking at her, Clarissa felt suddenly self-conscious. "I'm just glad to be here." She focused on her food, dipping her spoon into the alleged beef enchiladas.

As she listened to the friendly banter, turmoil tied her stomach in tight knots. Could she hope that Max's men had given up and gone back down the mountain? She couldn't finish this journey with the others and go back to Discovery, where Max would be waiting. She wasn't so sure she could make it on her own to the town Ezra had mentioned, but she had to try. If only she could get some specific instruction and directions.

After dinner, Ezra helped everyone pitch a small, single-man tent, except for Jan and Ken, who had a bigger tent to share. Clarissa said her good-nights and crawled into her sleeping bag. The cool night air came through the unzipped mesh windows.

Outside her tent, Ezra and Leonard talked in low tones until their voices faded, and she heard the unzipping of tent doors. The night quieted, but her mind raced with all that had happened and all that she had yet to do. Twice Clarissa grabbed her pack and unzipped the tent, thinking she would just escape in the night and take her chances. Both times she talked herself out of it. There was still so much more she needed to learn before she could face the wilderness on her own. She snuggled back down into the sleeping bag.

She listened for a long time, wondering if Leonard would get up in the night and drag her out of her tent.

She breathed in the fresh air as a light breeze rustled the nylon walls. Her eyelids grew heavy and she drifted off....

She awoke in total darkness to the sound of angry voices in the distance.

FIVE

Ezra awoke with a start, uncertain what had caused him to become alert. Was the noise something he had dreamed or something he'd heard? He reached into the tent pocket where he'd placed his flashlight. He unzipped the tent and leaned outside. The camp appeared quiet. The fire had died out. Trees creaked in the breeze. He shone a light on each of the tents.

Adrenaline surged through his veins when the beam revealed that Clarissa's tent door was unzipped. He crawled out of his tent and grabbed his shoes, hurrying over to shine the light in her open tent.

She was gone.

Ezra walked the perimeter of the camp, shining the light into the trees. Most likely she'd gotten up to go to the bathroom. He waited fifteen minutes, pacing around the camp and growing more concerned.

He returned to the tent, noting that her flashlight and her pack were still there. At least she'd thought to put shoes on before she left the safety of the camp. He couldn't wait any longer. She may have gotten hurt or not been able to find her way back. He strode through the forest, allowing the flashlight to illuminate the path in front of him.

It seemed foolhardy that she would be in such a big hurry that she wouldn't think to take the flashlight. He'd had clients do stupider things than that, but Clarissa struck him as far more sensible than most. He stopped running, shining the light into the darkness between trees. When he listened, only the creaking of the tree branches reached his ears. He strode onward, picking up his pace, circling the camp in an ever increasing perimeter.

After twenty minutes, he found some tracks and broken branches that indicated which direction she had gone, but still no sign of Clarissa.

Clarissa worked her way toward the sound of men talking, being careful to make as little noise as possible. She could hear the conversation now more distinctly. Any hope that they were just fellow backpackers was dashed when Don's gruff voice assaulted her eardrums.

Clarissa took in a breath to calm herself. She needed to make sure the men didn't hurt the others in her group. She had to distract them somehow, and lead them away. With the fire out, the camp was not visible through the trees. The two thugs would have to stumble into the tents before they discovered them.

In the dark, her footsteps were slow and careful, and she stretched a hand out in front of her. She could hear Don complaining about hunger and his aching feet. So the thugs hadn't come equipped for a hike that would take more than a few hours.

A light flashed among the trees, and she edged toward it. The second speaker became more distinct.

"He's paying us plenty for this. Let's get the job done." The voice sounded younger than Don's, but not one she recognized. Of course, Max would never go hiking in the woods. He'd pay someone to do it for him.

She dashed toward a tree with a large trunk and hid behind it. She angled around to get a look at the men. Don had a small flashlight, something that would be on the end of a key chain. He sat on a log, turned slightly sideways so she could see his profile. She didn't recognize the other man, who pulled a revolver from his waistband and opened and closed the cylinder. His red hair was distinctive in the minimal light.

Don took his shoe off and massaged his foot.

"How are we going to find her? We're talking thousands of acres."

"They stay on the trail. All we got to do is follow it until we catch up with them." The second thug peered down the barrel of his gun. "Besides, how perfect can this be? We do this right, get her separated from the group, no one will find her body out here for years—or at all. There are bears in these woods. They might just take care of her body for us."

Clarissa's throat constricted as she pressed her hand against the rough surface of the tree trunk. Fear coiled inside her, but she refused to give in to it. So they would find a way to separate her from the group and then kill her. That meant the two thugs probably wouldn't make themselves known to the rest of the group or hurt them. They didn't want witnesses or extra bodies. Could she hope to stay with the others and be safe?

Don rose to his feet and paced. "Man, I'd kill for a steak and fries right now."

"Let's get moving. Their camp has to be around here somewhere. We can pull her out of the tent before the others know what hit them," the younger man said. "Doing it in the dark is perfect. We need to get this done before first light."

"Yeah, if we can find where they're camped."

She watched the younger man shove his gun into his belt, the sneer on his hardened face visible in the faint light.

Don stomped around, stepping closer to where she was hidden. She angled around the tree out of sight, pressing her back against the rough texture of the bark and holding her breath.

"Hey, what was that?" Don's voice grew louder. His feet crunched across the fallen leaves on the forest floor.

She tensed. Had they heard her?

And then she heard it, too. Faintly in the distance. Ezra calling her name. The sound faded almost as quickly as it began.

"Did you hear that?" said the second man. "Let's check it out. It'll lead us to the camp."

Clarissa squeezed her eyes shut, and her whole body stiffened as she listened to the men moving through the forest away from her, toward the sound of Ezra's voice. She couldn't risk him being hurt. She pushed off from the tree and circled around the men, who were easy enough to pinpoint from their voices and the noise they made as they crashed through the forest.

She took in a breath and darted through the trees, picking up a branch and banging it against a log. She ran ahead several more feet, making sure to hit the branch against tree trunks and brush.

The men's voices had grown silent. She waited, listening, as her stomach jerked into her throat and her heart beat out an erratic rhythm. She heard their footsteps and hushed voices when they gave each other orders.

She stood her ground, watching. They had to see her, just for a split second, or they might not give chase. Every instinct told her she should run. She planted her feet and swallowed her fear. She couldn't hear Ezra's voice anymore, but that didn't mean he'd given up looking for her.

Tree branches shook. She could track their clumsy footsteps as they stomped through the underbrush. Thirty feet away, she saw the bobbing of the flashlight.

Don's voice pierced her like an arrow. "There she is. I see her."

Clarissa took off running. Moonlight illuminated only bits and pieces of the landscape. She zigzagged through the woods, nearly stumbling over a fallen log. She could hear the men behind her as though they were breathing down her neck. Her leg muscles strained as she slipped through the evergreens.

For at least twenty minutes, she could hear the thugs dogging her, pushing her to keep moving despite the fatigue. Slowly, though, their voices faded. She stumbled out into an opening. Down below, the ground grew steeper and rockier. She was sure they'd hiked through this area earlier in the day.

Clarissa found a large overhang of rock. Curling up underneath it, she wrapped her hands around her calves and leaned forward. The shadows covered her. If they managed to come this direction, they wouldn't see her here.

She waited, shivering in the nighttime cold, wondering if she'd die out here alone. She didn't know enough to keep herself alive. She needed Ezra's knowledge. But staying with the group put them all at risk.

Oh, God, help me, I don't know what to do.

In the predawn hours, she heard rocks rolling past her. When she peeked out, she saw the silhouettes of the two thugs as they moved back down the mountain. Hungry and ill-equipped, they'd given up for now. Neither of them seemed too crazy about being out in the wilderness. She had to hope that after their failure to find the group's camp, they would wait it out, thinking she would come back into Discovery with the others and they could grab her then.

She waited awhile longer and then pushed herself up the rocky hill. From there, she was able to find the river that led back to the camp.

It had to be three or four in the morning. All the tents except Ezra's were still zipped tight.

Driven by a sense of responsibility, he'd been out looking for her. As she crawled into her tent and slid into the sleeping bag, she wondered what she could say to him. How much did he need to know? This really was her problem, and she could handle it.

She zipped up the sleeping bag, allowing the warm down to surround her until her shivering stopped. A few minutes later she heard footsteps and the sound of Ezra getting back in his tent. She had slept for only a short time when she heard the clanging of pots banging against each other, and Ezra's voice calling out, "Rise and shine, everybody. It's time for breakfast."

Clarissa opened her eyes and stared at the roof of the tent, wishing she could continue to sleep. Ken's and Jan's groaning and lighthearted complaints reached her ears. She heard Leonard's voice and Bruce's, all of them joking with Ezra.

She sat up and wiggled out of the sleeping bag.

"Clarissa, come on, sleepyhead. We've got to get moving." The voice was Jan's.

Wishing she could snuggle back in bed and recover the hours of sleep she'd missed out on, she leaned forward and unzipped her tent door.

She crawled out of the tent and reached for her shoes. When she turned around, four sunny faces greeted her. Ezra stood off from the group, a look of betrayal clouding his features.

As he showed the others how to make coffee over the fire, Ezra could not let go of his suspicions about Clarissa. Where had she been all night? He'd finally given up on finding her, driven by his sense of duty to watch over the others. He was relieved when he came back and saw that she had returned to her tent.

He had to hand it to her. She must have wandered pretty far from the camp for him not to be able to find her. And yet she'd managed to navigate her way back in the dark. She'd demonstrated some innate survival skills. But why had she wandered off in the first place? He clenched his jaw. She'd popped her head out of the tent as though nothing had happened.

He'd heard the voices of the men in the forest. She must have had some sort of planned rendezvous with them. He could only guess at what she was up to. The deep woods provided the perfect hiding place for any number of illegal activities. He wanted to think the best of her, he really did. But she owed him an explanation bigtime. As soon as he could be alone with her, he had some questions that she needed to answer, for the safety of everyone else in the group.

He was stuck with her. They were too far into the hike to turn back. He couldn't leave the other clients to fend for themselves or cut their adventure short. And that meant that he needed to know what was going on—needed to know what steps he might have to take to protect everyone.

He watched as she rose to her feet and poured coffee into her metal cup. The dark circles under her eyes revealed the kind of night she'd had. She hadn't met his gaze since she'd stepped out of the tent.

"Everything all right?" Leonard slapped him on the back. "You look kind of upset."

Ezra pulled himself free of his speculation about Clarissa's motives for coming on the expedition. "Yeah, everything's fine." He took his eyes off her and addressed the whole group.

"Eat up. We've got a long day ahead of us. We'll break camp in twenty minutes."

They hiked through the day, stopping only briefly for lunch. The group stayed together for the most part, giving Ezra little opportunity to confront Clarissa.

Bruce walked beside him at one point, asking questions about hunting. Clarissa came up on the other side, holding a compass in her hand.

"Can you explain how this works? Like, say, I wanted to navigate to where that little town you mentioned was."

"The compass is so old-school," said Bruce, breathless from keeping pace with Ezra and talking at the same time. "Why aren't we using GPS?"

He addressed his answer to Bruce. "The idea is to get away from technology, keep it as primitive as possible without making it so unpleasant no one wants to come along with me." Ezra was grateful for the man's interruption. Clarissa's questions were starting to bother him. Why did she need to know how to navigate to New Irish?

Her questions earlier in the day had made more sense. She had wanted know the best places to find food, and how to catch small game. But all her inquiries came with such urgency. Most people relaxed when they got out here. She seemed more revved up than ever. He wanted to know what she was planning.

They hiked through the afternoon and made camp about a hundred yards from a river. The plan would be to teach them how to fish in the morning. "All right, people, let's see if we can forage to add to our meal."

"When are we going to learn how to get something with protein in it? I only have a couple more MREs left in my pack," Bruce said.

"Tomorrow morning we'll fish." Ezra turned toward the river. "Next day, I'll teach you how to catch rabbits and squirrels."

He watched the group divide up, the men going in one direction and the women in another. He doubted he was going to have any chance to talk to Clarissa alone before the day was over.

SIX

Clarissa breathed in the heady scent of coffee brewing as she crawled out of her tent. The others were already sitting around the fire, all of them smiling in welcome. Ezra stood a few feet away, holding his steaming metal coffee cup. She averted her gaze, not wanting to make eye contact with him. She'd managed to avoid being alone with him all day yesterday, so she wouldn't have to explain where she'd been in the night.

She'd toyed with the idea of telling him who those men were. But why involve him? This trouble was of her own making. She'd figure it out on her own. Ezra had a survival class to teach. She didn't want to disrupt that—especially when there was so much she could learn from it. The information could save her life when she was finally ready to strike out by herself. Thanks to his lessons, she now knew how to find and purify water. She could survive on roots and berries she found, for a couple days at least. If she could just get a bearing on how to get to the town Ezra had mentioned, she could strike out on her own.

"Good morning, sleepyhead," said Jan. She pulled the coffeepot from the fire and poured Clarissa a cup.

As she fished out a sugar packet from a plastic container, Clarissa regretted that she had to leave the group soon. She was starting to like these people. She hadn't spent much time with Leonard, still wary of his reasons for joining the expedition at the last minute, but the others were kind and fun.

Ezra returned to the group. "All right, people, finish up your coffee. This morning we're going to head down to the river to catch our breakfast."

Kenneth threw the remainder of his coffee toward the fire. "How long are we going to fish before we give up? My stomach's rumbling already."

Ezra offered them a wry grin. "Nothing like an empty stomach to motivate a man."

Clarissa smiled. Ezra really was a very good teacher. He had a way of gently pushing people to accomplish more than they thought they could.

Ezra took another sip of coffee. "If we are not

successful, don't worry. You still have MREs left in your pack. But the sooner you start to obtain your own food, the better."

"I'm glad we have that safety net," said Jan. She looped her arm through Clarissa's. Jan was so nice to her. They had a good time working together.

"I'm looking forward to this," said Bruce, rubbing his hands together. "I'm sure we'll do great."

The others finished their coffee and one by one headed down the mountain. Jan and Clarissa were the last to leave, taking time to put away the coffee and sugar. Jan set off toward the river ahead of her. Clarissa rose to her feet just as she heard a distinct mechanical noise. The helicopter was far off in the distance, a tiny black oval against the blue sky.

"Are you coming?" Jan shouted.

Clarissa caught up with her, then shaded her eyes from the morning sun as she gestured to the helicopter. "What do you suppose that is about?"

Her friend shrugged. "Ezra said there were other hikers around here. Maybe some of them get dropped off by helicopters, to start their hikes at a particular spot. Or maybe it's a search and rescue team doing an exercise."

From this distance, the aircraft didn't look

like it was marked as a rescue helicopter. It appeared solid black.

As they made their way toward the river, where the rest of the group waited, fear shook Clarissa from the inside. What if Don and the other thug had decided to search for her using a helicopter?

She couldn't wait any longer. As soon as the opportunity presented itself, she'd grab her pack and leave.

Ezra waited until Clarissa and Jan joined the group before he started talking. He braced himself for the anxious glances that passed between everyone. It happened every time he set up this lesson.

The rushing river water created background noise as he talked. The sky remained overcast and gray. He'd brought a rain poncho that fit in his pocket, in case the storm turned into something substantial. He wondered if anyone else had taken that precaution. If not, it would be a good lesson in planning ahead. The river was about twenty feet across, and over an average person's head in some spots.

Ezra cut a willow branch and started to sharpen the end with his knife while everyone watched him. "There are tons of different ways to catch fish other than using the overpriced fishing pole you can buy at a tourist trap sports shop."

The group laughed.

"Today, I will teach you two methods." He held up the finished willow stick. "You can spear the fish. Make sure you tie some cording around this to retrieve it."

"Where are we supposed to get the cording?" Bruce crossed his arms over his chest.

"Use a shoelace, whatever is available." Ezra then demonstrated how they could catch fish by luring them into a net with bait. "Okay, choose the method that you think you can be the most successful at. Look for the calm eddies where the fish are likely to congregate. We'll regroup back at the camp in two hours. Be aware of your surroundings, take note of the landmarks and don't wander too far from this point."

Bruce grabbed a willow branch from the bank and disappeared around the bend. Leonard and Ken walked away, their heads bent close together as they pointed at a smooth spot in the river.

Jan pulled Clarissa along the bank. They crossed the river on a fallen log and disappeared into a cluster of trees. He could hear the women laughing and talking. Their voices faded as they made their way up the rocky shore. Ezra was tempted to follow them, but decided against it.

Though he continued to look for a chance to talk to Clarissa, he had other clients to think about. He made his way in the opposite direction, up-river, to check on Bruce, who seemed insistent on doing everything alone. Ezra had to find a way to draw him back into the group.

He hiked a quarter mile with no sign of Bruce. The sky had turned a deeper shade of gray, and a few drops of rain landed on his shoulders. Shouts from downriver caused him to turn and run. He recognized Jan's screams, and he quickened his pace. The cries were coming from the other side, so he hurried over the log and strode toward them.

The screaming had stopped by the time he found Jan and Leonard huddled by the shoreline. Ken was dripping wet.

"Guess who fell in?" Ken offered Ezra a wry smile.

"Jan, take him up to the campsite. The fire should still be going. Get him dried off and warmed up. Where's Clarissa?"

Jan pointed farther downriver. "She wandered off that way. Said she needed quiet to catch the fish."

"Leonard, can you head upstream to find Bruce? We'll meet back at camp." Ezra stared down at the angled willow stick that held the one small fish Leonard had caught, then tilted his head, looking at the ominous dark clouds. "This storm is moving in fast. We might have to postpone the fishing lesson." Ezra pulled his rain poncho out of its tiny package and slipped it over his head.

Leonard handed the fish to Jan. "You can take this with you."

Ezra hurried down the river in search of Clarissa. Suspicion plagued his thoughts as he rounded bend after bend and didn't find her. Maybe she was meeting up with her "friends" again.

Lightning flashed in the sky, and the sprinkle of rain became a downpour. He continued along the bank, searching for Clarissa. His mission had changed from wanting to talk to her to knowing that he needed to get her back to the camp so the group could get prepared to deal with the storm, which was getting worse by the minute. They were going to have an impromptu lesson in staying warm and dry in a bad storm.

Clarissa looked around at the trees, trying to get her bearings. Rain soaked through her thin jacket. Once she'd broken away from Jan, her plan had been to travel far enough downriver to avoid notice, and then head back to the camp to retrieve her backpack. The thick brush she had to push through had gotten her turned around, muddling her sense of direction. She worked her way back to the river to try and figure out which way to go.

The water has risen and was rushing faster than ever. Chunks of debris floated by. Would she even be able to get back across on the log? As she stepped closer to the edge, a chunk of the muddy bank broke off. Clarissa slipped and her foot dipped into the river. Strong hands grabbed her and jerked her up. Ezra's arms enveloped her as he pulled her away from the bank. "Did your foot get wet?"

She nodded. Her hand rested against his chest as she looked into his deep brown eyes. Now how was she going to get away?

Lightning splintered the sky followed by the boom of thunder.

"That's pretty close. Let's get away from the water." He scanned the area around them. "If memory serves, there's a cattle shelter around here somewhere. My brothers and I used to play in it when we were kids."

Again lightning split the sky. This time it struck across the river, slicing through a tree and tossing it into the swirling water.

Clarissa pulled away from him. "Shouldn't we head back to camp?"

"Too far. We need to find someplace else to

wait the storm out." He started running before he'd finished his sentence.

Lightning struck directly behind them. The nearness of the blast rattled her nerves. She slipped her hand into Ezra's. He pulled her through the tangle of trees toward the shelter. The three-sided shed was in disrepair and leaned to one side, but at least it was a roof over their heads.

She slipped in beside him. "What is this place?"

"It's a shelter for cows to go into when the weather is bad. A lot of the land around here is government property that is leased out to ranchers. Must not be any cows running on it right now or they'd be in here with us."

Rain drizzled in from holes in the roof. Clarissa tilted her head and a drop fell on her face.

"Are you still getting wet?" He chuckled and pulled his poncho up, lifted the edge and stretched out his arm. "It's a little dryer under here."

She scooted under the shelter of the rain poncho, but still maintained some distance from him, uncomfortable with being so close.

"I can't hold my arm straight forever," he said.

She glanced at him and then edged nearer, close enough to feel his body heat. He adjusted the poncho so it covered them both. She pulled her knees up to her chest. Her wet foot felt like a block of ice. The downpour was so heavy that it looked like gray sheets of rain rather than drops. The opportunity to get away from the group was lost for now.

"I hope the others are okay," she said.

"Me, too. If they made it back to camp, they'll be able to keep warm and dry."

"I'm not sure if we'll be able to get back across the river." She couldn't hide the worry she felt.

"There's always a way, Clarissa," Ezra said.

She forced herself to smile. "That's right, we'll build a rope bridge with our shoelaces."

He laughed at her joke. "You don't need to worry. As soon as the rain lets up, we'll find a way across. Are you a little warmer?"

She nodded. "Yes, but my foot is still frozen."

"Take your shoe off, and I'll see if I can warm it up," he said.

She slid out of her hiking book and pulled the wet sock off. He gathered her foot into his hands. The warmth of his touch enveloped her.

"Better?" he asked after a while.

She nodded. The heat transmitted from his hands made her dizzy.

He let go of her foot. "Slip it into the boot. Don't put the sock back on. FYI, wool socks are better. They pull the moisture away from your skin."

After she put her boot back on, she sat listening to the rain, knowing that sooner or later Ezra was going to come around to asking her why she had left the tent two nights ago. She was trapped here with him until the rain stopped. It was no longer a question she could avoid. But how could she answer without admitting that she'd put him and the rest of the group in danger?

Ezra could feel her shivering next to him. He knew, though, that offering to wrap his arm around her for warmth would only send her to the other side of the shelter. The tension that filled the tiny space was almost palpable. She must sense that he wanted to ask her for an explanation of the shenanigans two nights ago. He dived in with both feet. "So who were those guys the other night?"

She hung her head. "They're after me. I don't know why, exactly. I think it has something to do with my former job in California."

Not the answer he had expected. "What did you do in California?" He braced himself for the answer and prayed that she would come clean with him.

She let out a heavy breath and shook her

head. "I was the assistant to a man who sold real estate and managed property. There must be something—something I saw, or overheard or something he thinks I know—that could get him in trouble. I don't know what it is, but it must be serious, since when I left California, he sent someone after me. The man at the airport is named Don. He works for my former boss, and he tried to abduct me as soon as I got off my flight. Then later that night, he tried to kill me. I joined the class to get away from him, but he followed me here. I overheard him in the woods two nights ago, talking with his partner. They were planning to snatch me from my tent. I let them spot me so I could lead them away from the camp and then hid out for most of the rest of the night."

In that moment, Ezra was struck by her vulnerability. She seemed to be telling the truth, which meant she hadn't been lying to him when she said she wasn't a criminal. Though that seemed to be his default position to explain her actions. Guilt washed over him.

"I didn't think they would find me out here." Her voice faltered. "I don't know if they'll be back or not. I was going to try to get away, so the others wouldn't be hurt. I think they just want me, but I don't know the extent to which they would go."

"Clarissa, why didn't you tell me in the first place?" Ezra leaned a little closer so he could see her face in the dim light. She stiffened but didn't pull away.

Her eyes searched his. "It's my mess. I'm the one who needs to deal with it."

"You don't have to do everything on your own. What makes you think I wouldn't have understood?"

She rested her forehead against her hand. "I know I made it worse by thinking I had to fix it on my own. I see that now, and I worry that those guys might hurt someone to get to me."

Ezra cleared his throat. "There is the rest of the group to think about." He wasn't sure how to solve this problem. His responsibility wasn't only to her.

Outside, the rain continued to fall, creating puddles around the wood structure. She was still shivering.

"If you pull some of this loose straw around you, it'll warm you up a little."

She gathered the straw around her lower body.

"Here, hold this." He transferred the poncho to her and bunched up the remaining straw around her. "Take your wet jacket off." Then he removed his flannel shirt, which was still dry, and draped it over her shoulders. All he had on now was his long-sleeved T-shirt.

Gratitude shone in her eyes as she slipped out of the wet jacket and into the flannel shirt. "Aren't you going to get cold?"

"I'll be all right." He pulled the poncho over his shoulders. "Long as I keep dry."

The rain fell relentlessly, and the puddles outside grew larger and deeper. He spoke some about growing up with his four brothers and his time as a marine. Clarissa offered only yes and no answers to his questions about her life.

Gradually, though, she eased closer to him, seeming to trust him more, until their shoulders were touching, and he could feel her body heat through his thin cotton shirt.

She spoke up. "I don't know if those men will come back for me or not."

He was glad she trusted him enough to share her concerns.

"Maybe once this storm lets up and we are all back together, the group can be told the situation and then decide whether they want to continue or head back down the mountain."

"Really? We're going to involve everyone?"

"Those people care about you already. Jan treats you like you're her long-lost daughter."

Clarissa turned to face forward, obviously thinking deeply about what he had said.

"All of this is because of me. It's me they're after. I'm the one who should head back down the mountain." Despite the resolve in the words, he could hear that her voice was filled with fear.

"Clarissa, we make these decisions as a team."

"Maybe you could point me toward that little town you said was on the other side of the mountain. I think I would be safe there."

"It would be irresponsible of me to send you off alone. What kind of a man do you think I am?"

"It's just that all these people paid for a wilderness adventure, and my problems shouldn't get in the way of that. I don't know if those men will even come back." Her eyes glazed with tears and he was struck by the guilt that he saw there.

His fingers grazed her cheek, and he spoke more tenderly. "We'll figure this out together as a group."

The drone of the rainfall was interrupted by a cry. Both of them turned to face outward.

She gripped his upper arm. "Was that human?"

He leaned out a little more, listening and studying the landscape. They were surrounded by trees except for a path that led back to the river. Another cry rose up. This one was more distinct, but still far away.

"That might be one of our group. I have to go check it out."

She moved to follow him.

"You stay here."

"But it's raining buckets out there. You'll get wet." She moved to take off the shirt.

"Keep it. I'll take the poncho." He slipped into it and put up the hood while he crouched beneath the roof of the shelter.

Rain gushed over him as he stepped out into the wind. He looked back to see Clarissa huddled with her legs drawn up to her chest and her head down. She wouldn't stay dry for long with that leaky roof. He found some fallen tree branches and placed them on the roof, then bent over and looked in at her. "That should help keep you dry."

She hugged her knees with her arms. "Thank you."

"Promise me you'll stay here until I get back. This is the safest place for you until this storm lets up."

He heard another cry. This time he could discern the word *help*. The sound was coming from upriver. "Promise me, Clarissa."

She looked up at him and nodded. That look in her eyes was like that of an animal caught in a trap, filled with desperation.

"I'll come back for you. Just stay here."

With only a backward glance, Ezra plodded toward the river. The water had risen and was rushing even faster. He made his way along the bank toward where he'd heard the call for help.

He prayed that he'd make it in time to rescue whoever was crying out, and that the others were safe and dry on high ground. More than anything he prayed that Clarissa would stay put until he could come back for her, and wouldn't think she had to go off on her own.

SEVEN

Clarissa slipped back into a corner of the shelter where it didn't seem to be leaking as much. She gathered the straw around her. Her shivering had subsided thanks to Ezra's warm flannel shirt. The heat from his body had seeped through her skin when she'd put it on. His kindness had caught her off guard.

He'd been angry at her deception, and rightly so. But the care he took with her, making sure she was safe and dry, confused her. Sending her packing down the mountain alone after what she had done would have made more sense to her. She had hurt his business and could have jeopardized the safety of the others in the group.

Max Fitzgerald was not Ezra Jefferson's problem. And yet he was willing to take it on. What if Max's thugs did come back? The memory of Jan helping her, of laughing and joking with her, caused guilt to wash over Clarissa again. She couldn't risk harm to these good people.

After ten minutes, the rain finally showed signs of letting up. She dived out into it, determined to find a way across the river and over the mountain. The water had risen several inches and was rushing fast. She remembered the log where she and Jan had crossed in the first place and ran in that direction, seeking the cover of the trees as much as possible. When she came to the log, she found it completely submerged. Clarissa stood with the wind and rain whipping around her, and tried to fight off a feeling of despair. There had to be another way across.

She retreated deeper into the trees to escape the worst of the storm while still following the river. She heard what she thought was Ezra's voice, though it blended with the wind. Maybe it was only her hopeful heart. She didn't know what to do with the kind of consideration he had shown her. Part of her did not want to leave him or the group even though she knew she had to.

She walked farther upriver, bent over to resist the worst of the storm. When she poked her head through the trees to assess crossing the rapidly moving water, she saw a flash of color ahead of her: Ezra's rain poncho hanging on a tree. Fearing the worst, she ran toward it.

Ezra stood in the raging water, holding on to Bruce's upper body.

"Hurry, I can't hold him much longer. His

arm is trapped underneath a log," he shouted above the roar of the river. "Find something you can use to wedge it off of him."

Clarissa turned in a half circle, searching for a strong branch. She ran a short distance toward one, but quickly dismissed it—too weak. Bruce's cries of agony pelted her ears. She dragged a crooked branch from beneath some thick underbrush and rushed back to the river.

Freezing water swirled around her as she waded in beside Ezra.

"Hold his head out of the water. I'll lift the log off," he told her.

Clarissa handed Ezra the stick and nestled her hands underneath Bruce's head, lifting it above the rushing water. He opened his eyes, but no light of recognition shone in them when he looked at her. His skin was so pale it appeared almost translucent. His lips were blue.

Ezra stepped through the river, bending at the waist and feeling for Bruce's arm and the log that pinned him down. He jabbed the branch into the water, then strained against it, groaning. "Now! Get him out now!"

Clarissa wrapped her arms around Bruce's chest and pulled backward, nearly falling into the water herself. Ezra braced her back with his arm and then gripped Bruce. They dragged the man toward safety before collapsing on the rocky shore. Bruce took in a sputtering breath and turned to one side.

Ezra gazed up the hillside. "All of us need to get warmed up quickly. Let's get back to the campsite. The others must have gone there already."

Clarissa reached out to help Bruce to his feet, but his knees buckled as soon as he stood. Ezra slipped in beside the injured man and rested Bruce's rubbery arm on his shoulder.

It took only seconds for the cold air to hit her skin. Her teeth chattered as they made their way up the hill. Finally, the camp came into view.

"I'll build a fire. You take care of his arm. Do you know how to dress a wound?"

Clarissa nodded. "From first aid classes."

Ezra was already racing around the camp, pulling his pack out of the tent and slipping into a fresh flannel shirt.

Clarissa saw no sign of Jan or Ken or Leonard. Where could they be? The camp looked out of order. One of the tents was missing, maybe blown away by the storm. Another had collapsed.

Bruce groaned in pain, and Clarissa drew her attention back to him. He held his arm protectively against his chest. She poked her head inside one of the tents, which looked relatively dry. "Bruce, can you get in here to stay warm?"

While he crawled into it, Ezra pulled a tarp out of his tent. "Help me get this up so we can get out of the rain and build a fire," he told Clarissa.

They worked quickly, grabbing sturdy sticks to prop up the tarp. He dashed in and out of the camp, piling up wood and kindling. "Some of this will be dry enough to burn." He pulled items from his pack. "We need to find anything dry that will burn. Any kind of paper."

After she helped Ezra find kindling, Clarissa grabbed a piece of cloth and some string from her pack. When she glanced up again at Ezra, he had a fledgling fire started.

"It's kind of hard. Everything is so wet."

She nodded in understanding, then called out toward the tent where she'd left their patient. "Bruce, we got a fire started, and a tarp set up so we'll be out of the rain. Come on out, and I can put your arm in a sling." At least she hoped she could. She'd done something like this only once, in a first aid class.

Bruce poked his head out of the tent, pressed his lips together and nodded. He crawled out, and Clarissa was pleased to note that he'd started to get a little color back into his face. "I've got a cut on my leg, too," he said.

She touched his arm as gently as she could. His body jerked and he let out a groan. Her hands were trembling from cold as she draped the cord around his neck and tied it through a hole she'd punched in the cloth.

"Let me see the cut on your leg," she said.

Bruce lifted his pant leg. Clarissa winced when she saw the gash. She located the first aid kit, put disinfectant on the cut and covered it with gauze and medical tape.

She helped Bruce to his feet and settled him in front of the fire.

"Stay close to the heat. Get dried out." She patted his shoulder. He nodded.

She felt the weight of a blanket settling on her shoulders, and Ezra leaning close and whispering in her ear. "Now get yourself warmed up."

She settled down beside Bruce while Ezra disappeared into the trees and returned with more wood. He tossed it beside the fire. "Once we get it going strong, we can throw some of that damper wood on." He knelt and held his hands closer to the flames.

"Where is everybody?" Bruce's voice was weak.

"I don't know. I'm not sure what happened here."

Clarissa detected the tension woven into Ezra's words. His sideways glance toward her made her wonder if the reason for the others' disappearance wasn't the storm, but something more sinister. Something connected to her.

Ezra allowed the heat from the flames to surround him. His pants were soaked, and he was still shivering. There were a hundred things he needed to do, but he would be no good to anyone if hypothermia overtook him. His mind raced. He wasn't sure about Leonard, but Jan and Ken should have been at the camp. So where were they?

He couldn't focus on the disaster that was behind him. He needed to put his energy into pulling things back together. He needed to find the other members of the group. Clearly, Bruce couldn't continue the journey. And they all might need to be going home. The first step was to get some help on the way with the satellite phone.

Bruce lay down close to the fire and nodded off. The rain had turned into a drizzle.

Clarissa patted the sleeping man's shoulder. "He's been through a lot."

"We all have. This was certainly not what was on the itinerary."

She stared at the disaster that had been their camp, a sad and bewildered expression on her face. She drew the blanket tighter around her shoulders.

If it hadn't been for Clarissa showing up when she did, he might not have been able to save Bruce. "Thanks for helping me back there."

She stared at the fire. "It's what anyone would have done."

"Guess I'm glad you left that shelter after I told you not to." That much was true…but it led to the question he wished he didn't have to ask. "Where were you headed?"

She opened her mouth as though to say something, but then turned sideways, pulling the blanket tighter around her. She focused on the flames, touching the back of her neck delicately, and then looked out into the distance.

"You weren't thinking about taking off on your own, were you?"

She stared down at her hands. "I've been so much trouble already."

Ezra leaned toward her, taking her face in his hands. "I meant what I said. We decide as a group how to deal with your problem."

She cupped her fingers over his, the warmth of her touch seeping through his skin. The furrow between her brows indicated he still hadn't got through to her.

If kindness didn't work, maybe he could scare her into not bolting. "You'll die out there by yourself." Or guilt her into staying. "I don't want that on my conscience." His hand pressed against her cheek and he brushed away a strand of wet hair. The look of disbelief remained on her face.

He moved back. "Look, we might not be staying out here, depending on what condition Jan and Ken and Leonard are in when I find them. First things first. I've got to get on that satellite phone and get some help for Bruce."

Ezra stuck his head back in his tent. The phone wasn't there.

Clarissa must have picked up on his alarm when he poked his head back out. "Is something wrong?"

He looked all around the area. Rain pattered on his skin as he surveyed the campsite. The phone was not anywhere. He didn't want to scare Clarissa, so he decided to keep the news to himself for now. In the meantime, he had to think in terms of getting everyone to a safe place, which was proving to be harder by the minute.

"I'm going to do a quick survey around here and down by the river to see if I can find the others, or at least figure out where they went." And search some more for the satellite phone. He pulled a meal packet from his pack. "You should focus on eating something and getting food into Bruce."

"How long will you be gone?" Clarissa's voice was tinged with fear.

"Less than an hour." He moved toward her. "I do need you to stay put this time."

Ezra walked the perimeter of the camp in widening circles. The only sign he found of the others was a canteen that must have fallen from one of the packs. So they had headed uphill, maybe seeking better shelter. From his trained perspective the move was a foolish one. Once the storm was raging, the smart thing to do would be to hunker down in the camp, not hope to find something better when you didn't know the lay of the land. But Ken and Jan hadn't had that training. Was it possible that they had panicked and taken the satellite phone with them?

Ezra picked up the canteen and turned it over. He wondered, too, if something or someone had driven them out of the camp. They'd taken their packs, but left tents and sleeping bags behind, signs of a hurried retreat.

He walked down to the river to the last place he'd seen Leonard. He found no sign of the older man. When he returned to camp, Bruce was sitting up and shoveling a plateful of beans into his mouth. The color had returned to his skin and he seemed alert.

"I've got some hot food if you want." Clarissa

stirred the pot on the fire. "It's just rehydrated beans with some kind of mystery meat in it."

Ezra grabbed a tin plate. She filled it with several spoonfuls of beans.

"No sign of them?" she asked. He could tell she was trying not to sound worried.

"I think they may have headed uphill." He glanced around, pushing down the growing anxiety. "Why, I don't know."

"Maybe they got scared when that storm came up." She spooned out some food for herself. Her movements were quick and jerky. She was on edge, too. Maybe they were both thinking the same thing. That it wasn't the storm that had driven Jan and Ken, and maybe even Leonard, out of the camp.

Ezra addressed his question to Bruce. "Did you see the others at all?"

Bruce rested his spoon on the edge of the plate. "I heard Leonard calling for me. We never caught up with each other." He shook his head. "My big mistake was that I kept trying to catch fish even after the storm got so bad. That's why I fell into the river."

Bruce had beaten himself up enough over the accident. What he needed now was encouragement so he wouldn't stay in that place of condemnation. "This storm wasn't even a factor when I checked the seven-day forecast," Ezra told him. "It's not something we could plan for and certainly not something I adequately prepared you for."

They ate, then packed up what they could carry, leaving several of the tents behind in case the others came back and needed them. At this point they were closer to the lodge than the trailhead and the van. Ezra had decided to lead them up the trail toward the lodge, searching for the others along the way. Once they reached the lodge, they could radio for a helicopter for Bruce. With any luck, Ezra wouldn't also have to be asking for a search party for three people.

By early evening, fatigue set into Clarissa's legs. Bruce seemed to be slowing down, as well. He favored the leg that had the cut on it. They'd hiked at a steady pace, stopping as little as possible. When he did call for a break, Ezra would leave the trail to search for Jan and the others. In all, he'd probably hiked twice as much as she and Bruce had. He left cloth markers ripped from Jan and Ken's distinctive yellow tent on trees, so if the others were behind them, they would know Ezra had come this way.

Clarissa hooked her thumbs under the straps of her pack and quickened her pace to catch up with Ezra. "Should we be stopping to make camp soon?"

He paused and stared at the sky. "I'd like to press on for a long as we can."

He hadn't said much since breaking camp, and when he did, he kept his comments positive. She appreciated how he was trying to keep up morale, but the weight of the worry he carried was evident in his demeanor. His silence spoke volumes about how grave he thought the situation was.

Ezra had a sort of inner core of strength she had never encountered in a man before. His fortitude boosted her confidence that everything would turn out right and kept her own worry at bay.

They hiked until hours past dark. Finally, it was clear that Bruce, worn out from his accident and the pain of his injuries, could not continue.

"Most everything is still wet from the storm," Ezra reminded them. "We'll dry it out overnight, and you guys will have an impromptu lesson in building shelters from your surroundings."

Once the shelter was up and the fire started, Ezra grabbed a flashlight from his pack.

"Are you going out searching some more?" Clarissa rose to her feet. He shouldn't have to carry this load alone.

He seemed pensive. "Thought I'd give a quick look around and see if I can set some rabbit traps."

"Two sets of eyes are better than one," she said.

"I can handle cooking dinner." Bruce pulled open his pack. "I can at least be useful in that way."

The flames danced across Ezra's face as he considered her proposition. "All right, come with me. Does your flashlight still work?"

She retrieved it and followed him into the thick forest. They walked side by side.

"How far are we from the lodge?"

"We got a late start today. I'd say a long day's hike from here. We'll leave at first light. Bruce is cooking up the last of the rations tonight. Empty stomachs will only slow us down. If we can catch something tonight, we won't have to stop along the way."

They stepped into a part of the forest with a lot of brush. He showed her how to build a twitch-up snare to catch rabbits and other small game.

"Now it's your turn," he said. "You pick a spot where you think the rabbits might be and build a trap."

She smiled at him. "You just never stop being the teacher, do you?"

His voice became serious. "It's not a lesson at this point, Clarissa. We're in the midst of a real-life survival situation."

She'd tried to lighten the mood, but he'd spoken the words that had flirted around the corners of her mind all day.

He rested a hand on her shoulder. "While you do that, I'm going to have a look around. See if there's any sign that the others came this way. I won't go far."

Clarissa listened to Ezra's footsteps fade as she worked in the waning light to tie the parachute cord and bend the branch that served as a trigger mechanism. Wind rushed through the trees, and she could hear the sound of her own breathing.

She clicked on the flashlight, placed it in her mouth and focused it on the knot she struggled to tie. When she looked up it was even darker. Silence fell like a heavy shroud around her.

Ezra should have been back by now. She rose to her feet, her heart fluttering in her chest. She stepped in the direction he'd gone and then paused, remembering her promise to wait where he'd left her. A gust of wind rushed over the grass as she watched the darkening trees.

Maybe it was some primitive instinct kicking in, but the forest at night held a foreboding feeling for Clarissa. A chill ran over her skin as she had the sense that she was being watched.

"Ezra?" She waited. The sound of her own breathing surrounded her, seemingly louder in the tense silence. She turned in a half circle, waiting for him to emerge through the trees.

She returned to check her snare, focusing her energy on something that would help get her mind off the fear. Ezra should be back any minute.

She checked the tension of her string. A cracking sound reached her ears, a branch breaking.

Clarissa shot to her feet, uttering Ezra's name again. If he didn't answer this time, she'd leave. She wasn't going to wait around here any longer. He'd figure out that she'd headed back to camp.

She strode toward the tree line and entered the thick evergreens. Moments later she heard footsteps to one side. She saw a flash of Ezra's plaid shirt before he stepped out onto the trail.

"Hey," he said, then reached out for her. He must have seen the fear in her expression.

She pulled away from him. "What took you so long?"

"I kept looking, thinking I'd find some sign of them. I lost track of time."

"You shouldn't have left me alone out there." She was defensive, but the quaver in her voice gave away how afraid she'd been.

He stepped closer to her. "I'm sorry. I know that the forest at night can be kind of scary for someone who doesn't spend a lot of time in it."

The warmth in his voice comforted her. "We should have met back at camp." She crossed her arms over her chest, still maintaining a tone of offense, though she felt herself weakening.

"I won't ever put you in a dangerous situation or give you something you can't handle. You're stronger than you know, Clarissa." He patted her back and rested a hand on her shoulder.

She tilted her head to meet his gaze. Even as the heat of his touch soaked through to her bones, her heart retreated, running a hundred miles an hour. She reminded herself that men never meant what they said. Men broke their promises.

"Let's get back to the camp," she murmured.

He fell in behind her. When they arrived, Bruce spooned up three plates of hot food for them. By the time they'd finished eating it was completely dark.

"We should get some sleep," Ezra announced. "Four or five hours and then we need to get moving."

They slipped into the makeshift lean-to. Clarissa pulled the dry sleeping bag up around her. On the other side of the shelter, the breathing of the two men grew heavy with sleep. She stared at the woven branches of the roof, tired beyond belief, but still unable to sleep as anxiety made her thoughts race.

Bruce let out a cry of pain in his sleep. He needed medical attention. His leg might be getting infected. Part of her wondered if they should have turned back and gone down to the van instead of pushing forward to the lodge. Would the lodge have the medical supplies Bruce needed? And would they be able to contact anyone to send help? If they'd gone back to the van, at least they'd be able to drive back to town. The lodge would place them even farther from civilization.

But deep down, Clarissa knew that Ezra had made a sound decision in a tough situation. They faced so many unknowns. He could only work with what they knew to be true—that the lodge was closer and easier for them to reach, especially given Bruce's condition. Besides, Ezra had an obligation to the others, as well. Maybe Ken, Jan and Leonard had just gone on ahead to the lodge. They had a compass and knew the general direction.

Clarissa turned over on her side, still unable to let go of the dark thoughts that plagued her. The only thing that steadied her nerves was knowing that Ezra would do everything he could to keep them alive and get them to a safe place. She only hoped it would be enough.

EIGHT

Ezra awoke in the darkness. When he sat up, he saw that the fire had become glowing embers. He unzipped his sleeping bag and slipped into his shoes. Bruce slept fitfully beside him.

Ezra was grateful to see the outline of Clarissa's body across the shelter. Her default reaction seemed to be to run. She'd been on the run when she'd stowed away in his van. She'd evaded whoever was after her by coming on the expedition, and she'd gotten a notion to take off during the storm.

Tonight, though, she had chosen to stay. Progress…maybe.

As he gathered firewood and rooted through the pack for any remnants of coffee or tea, he wondered again what kind of life Clarissa had had. He wanted to know more about her.

Once the fire was going and he'd collected water from the creek to boil, he wandered out in the early-morning light to check the trap.

His efforts yielded one medium-sized rabbit. He knelt in the open field, gutting and skinning the animal. Noises emanated from the surrounding trees. Probably a deer waking to find some food. Though the deer never made an appearance in the open meadow, the noise continued.

Once he'd finished with the rabbit, he rose to his feet and headed back toward the camp. Clarissa sat in front of the fire, the sleeping bag still draped over her shoulders. Her cheeks were rosy from being so close to the heat, and her eyes were full of light. "We made it through the night."

"Yeah."

Her expression changed when he stepped closer. He stared down at the blood on his shirt and then held up the rabbit. "Food for the day."

"Ooh." She grimaced and jerked back.

He laughed. "You won't be complaining when it fills your belly." He glanced over at Bruce, who was still sleeping. "You'd better wake him up. We have to get moving."

Clarissa roused Bruce, who remained groggy even after coffee and breakfast. His injuries seemed to be getting the best of him.

Ezra asked, "How is your leg doing, Bruce?"

Bruce sat beside Ezra and peeled back the bandage Clarissa had put on his leg. She winced. The area around the cut was red…not a good sign.

Ezra patted Bruce on the back and tried to sound upbeat. "You'll be all right, buddy. Make sure you get some ibuprofen in you from the first aid kit."

Clarissa, who had been watching, said, "I can redress that wound for you if you like." She managed to wipe the worried expression off her face when Bruce looked at her, but Ezra had seen it.

Clarissa cleaned the dishes with a damp rag while Ezra doused the fire after he had packed up the cooked rabbit meat. She helped Bruce slip his lighter pack over his shoulders. Ezra held up Clarissa's pack for her. She clipped the straps into place.

He'd spent all of breakfast trying to keep the dark thoughts at bay. In a survival situation, most of the battle was mental. Ezra needed to focus on the possibility of good outcomes, not ugly ones.

Clarissa offered him a quick smile of encouragement before falling in behind Bruce. They had traveled only a short distance from the campsite when a woman's screams shattered the quiet of the forest.

Jan's shrill cries for help were like a sword slicing through Clarissa's torso. She took off running in the direction of the noise. Her pack slowed her down, so she dumped it on the ground and sprinted through the trees. Ezra ran past her.

They found Jan tied to a tree and blindfolded. Clarissa's heart surged with empathy. How could anyone do this to this kind woman? She ran to Jan, removing the blindfold and cupping her face in her hands.

Jan spoke between tears. "I'm so glad to see you."

Ezra cut the ropes. Clarissa wrapped her arms around Jan, and she fell into them, sobbing.

Clarissa glanced around, and then at Ezra, whose worried look fueled her own fears. Where were Ken and Leonard?

As she waited for the sobbing to let up and Jan to pull away, Clarissa continued to scan the area for whoever might have done this. The rustling sound of someone approaching made her tense, but it was only Bruce catching up with them.

She continued to hold Jan, keeping her arm around the older woman's shoulder. "What happened?" She blurted the question and braced for the answer, knowing that it had to be connected to the men who were looking for her.

Jan wiped the tears from her dirt-stained face. Her clothes were muddy, as well. Clarissa could only imagine what she'd been through.

Bruce and Ezra moved in closer.

Clarissa squeezed Jan's shoulder.

"Ken and I left the campsite, thinking we could get to a dryer spot. We ran into two men. They took us because they couldn't find Clarissa. They blindfolded us right away. I never got a good look at them." Jan's breathing quickened as she stared at the ground. "They brought me here. They're holding Ken. They said...they will trade Ken for Clarissa."

Jan closed her eyes as her entire body shuddered. "They promised there won't be any trouble. That's the message I'm supposed to give you."

So the men had upped their game, probably out of desperation or pressure from Max. Clarissa felt as if she were sinking in quicksand. Her muscles went numb. This was all because of her.

"What about Leonard? Where's Leonard?" Bruce pressed closer.

Jan stared at him. Her eyes glazed as she shook her head. "I don't...know. We never saw him after the storm."

Clarissa lifted her chin. "Where are they?"

"We're not going to make that kind of exchange." Defiance colored Ezra's words.

"But I have to. I have to save Ken." Clarissa raised her voice as guilt washed over her.

"When I agreed to take the five of you on the

expedition, I signed on to keep all of you safe."
Ezra spoke with a note of authority that made
it hard for her to respond.

"But Ken is only in danger because of me."
Clarissa's voice was barely above a whisper.

"I wouldn't want to see you hurt, either," said
Jan, reaching out and stroking her arm.

Clarissa looked at the older woman, amazed.
She shook her head. After all Jan must have
gone through, she wasn't mad at her? How was
that possible?

Jan squeezed Clarissa's upper arm. "I heard
those men talking. I know you haven't done
anything wrong."

Ezra turned to face Jan. "Where are they
holding him?"

She reached into her pocket. "They gave me
a map. They expect you there within the hour."

Ezra stared at the map. He must be formulating some sort of plan. "What about the satellite phone?"

Jan shook her head, not understanding.

"It was missing when we got back to the
camp," he explained. "I thought maybe you had
it with you."

She shook her head again. "We didn't take it."

"They must have taken it or destroyed it." Ezra
paced back and forth, his expression serious.

Clarissa let the words sink in. Fear rattled

her body from the inside. That phone was their way of reaching help. They were cut off from the world.

Ezra planted his feet. "Bruce, I need for you, Clarissa and Jan to head due north on the trail. The lodge is half a day away. Radio for help as soon as you get there."

Bruce nodded. "I can handle that."

"No," said Clarissa. "I'm going with you. We're going to make the exchange."

Jan gave Clarissa a hug. "Ezra knows what he's doing. It wouldn't be right to turn you over to those terrible men."

Ezra didn't respond. Instead, he pulled out the scraps of rations and the cooked rabbit he had left in his pack and handed them to Bruce. "You'll be able to find water along the way."

It looked like Ezra had made up his mind, but she wasn't about to give up without a fight. "At least let me go with you and help you so it's not one against two. I'm the one that's in the best shape physically to help you."

After brushing his hand over his face, he stared at her for a long moment.

"She has a point," Jan said.

"Okay," he conceded. "But I'm not putting anyone in jeopardy on purpose. Understood?"

"Understood." She'd do whatever Ezra said—

but she wasn't about to have Ken pay for her poor judgment.

He turned to face Bruce again. "You'll need to move slower because of your injury. We should be able to catch up with you."

If they weren't killed.

Bruce and Jan headed up the trail, disappearing around a bend into the trees.

Ezra glanced at the map and folded it. "We don't have much time. We need to move on this."

Clarissa grabbed his arm. "I never meant to be the cause of all this trouble."

"I know. Clarissa, you've got to let go of your guilt. You need to focus on the present. You and I are the strongest ones in the group right now."

"I just think it would be easier if I turned myself over to them."

She could tell Ezra was getting frustrated with her. "Do you really think they'll keep their word and not hurt Ken?" he asked.

She didn't know how to answer that. Certainly, the men didn't want a bloodbath. With her lack of ties, Clarissa would be easily disposed of, but Ken probably had plenty of family and friends who would cause a fuss if he went missing. Surely Max didn't want to have to deal with that. "I don't know what they're capable of. I just know that none of this would be happening if I hadn't—"

He grabbed her arms above the elbow. "The why of this doesn't matter. What we need to focus on is getting everybody out of here alive. Let it go and look ahead to the next thing you have to do, Clarissa."

His gaze was so intense she felt as if he was looking right into her soul.

"That guilt will consume you if you let it. Wash it from your mind. Jan and Bruce were in no condition to help me. I need your A-game here."

Clarissa nodded, the only response she could manage at the moment. The power of his words rendered her speechless. Ezra was depending on her. The group was depending on her. A single tear trailed down her cheek.

His eyes searched her as her cheeks flushed with heat. "You're not a throwaway in this life. You matter, too, Clarissa."

Her lips parted as she prepared to protest.

He wrapped his arms around her waist and pulled her toward him. He kissed her full on the mouth. "When are you going to get it through your head that people care about you? I care about you." He jerked away and strode up the trail.

Stunned, she stepped in behind him. The heat

from his lips pressing on hers lingered, sending a warm sensation over her skin. But it was his words that had her reeling.

You matter, too, Clarissa.

She trudged forward, staring at his back. What was he thinking right now? What had that kiss even been about? Ezra Jefferson was not the kind of man who ever revealed his fear. But he had to be worried about how they were going to pull this off. Maybe the kiss had been about his own fear and needing some assurance from her.

She did believe in him as a leader, but maybe he needed to hear that. She hurried to catch up with him. "I think you and I can do this, Ezra. We can rescue Ken."

Ezra trudged forward, looking straight ahead. "Tell me everything you know about these men."

"One of them I've never met. The other is Don. He has a temper, carries a gun and tried to strangle me. He's muscular and strong, but he's not in any kind of shape to run a long distance. When I overheard them talking the other night, I got the sense that neither one of them had ever spent much time in the woods."

Ezra didn't react to what she'd told him. His only response was to walk faster. "When we get close to their location, we'll move in slow to watch them. That way we can figure out the best plan of attack."

"I'll do whatever you say," she said.

He stuttered in his step and finally made eye contact with her. "Thank you for not working against me."

Despite her confidence in Ezra, each step deeper into the forest resulted in an ever-increasing weight on her. What if someone died at her expense? She'd never forgive herself.

"So why are these guys after you anyway?"

"If I knew that I might be able to settle things with them. Max sent them. As his assistant, I handled a lot of his financial and logistical information. I scheduled his meetings and sat in on some of them. I keep going over in my mind everything I did for those few weeks that I held the job, and I can't come up with anything that would be worth killing me over. He must think I know something that I don't."

Ezra slowed his pace, turning from side to side. He lowered his voice. "We're getting close."

A heavy weight seemed to press on her chest and her legs turned to rubber. Clarissa took in a deep breath, determined not to give in to her fear. What Ezra had said was right. She had to let go of the guilt and stop obsessing over how things could have been different. She would only hurt the rest of the group more if she didn't.

"The place where they're waiting is by a rocky outcropping." He spoke in a whisper. "They'll be expecting you to show up to make the exchange, so we won't have the element of surprise on our side." He spoke slowly, as though mulling over plans and possibilities.

He placed his fingers over his lips, indicating that they needed to be quiet. He pointed ahead through the trees. Both of them stepped more carefully over the soft undergrowth. She edged closer to him, ducking under low branches.

A patina of sweat formed on her forehead. She found it difficult to take in a deep breath.

Ezra held up his hand, indicating that they needed to stop. She pressed close to him and looked through the framework of trees where he was focused. She couldn't see anything. Slowly, though, human voices separated themselves out from the noises of the forest.

Ezra dropped to his hands and knees and inched his way toward the voices, using the trees for cover. Being careful not to break fallen branches, Clarissa eased in behind him, peering over his shoulder.

The man she didn't know sat on a rock while Don paced. Her heart lurched when she saw

Ken some distance from the fire, hands tied behind his back, face contorted by anguish.

She willed herself not to give in to the guilt. *It won't help us get him out of here.*

Don checked his watch. "Where is she?"

The second thug pulled his gun out of his waistband, pushing the cylinder of his revolver in and out and then spinning it. "Give it time, man. We have options even if she doesn't show." He looked over at Ken.

A shiver ran down Clarissa's spine. It was clear what they had to do, and quickly. She backed away, retreating, until she knew they were a safe distance from the two men.

"We have to hurry," she said. "I don't want to think about what they have planned for Ken."

Ezra nodded. "They're both armed."

"What if I'm bait? I'll step out…"

Ezra opened his mouth to protest. She placed her fingers on his lips to silence him. She spoke forcefully, knowing this was the only option that had any chance of working. "I'll say that I've come to make the exchange, and that I've come alone. Hopefully, they will untie Ken and let him go. Then—" she took in a breath to calm her nerves "—I get away and you help me."

"That's too dangerous for you."

"What other options do we have?"

He considered. "What if they don't let Ken go?"

"We improvise," she said.

Ezra took a long time to answer. He cupped her shoulder. "I'll be close. You won't see me, but I'll be there."

She nodded, even as panic welled up in the pit of her stomach. "Let's do this."

Clarissa stepped through the trees, fearing that her legs would collapse beneath her. When she looked behind her, she couldn't see Ezra anymore. She had to trust that he was watching and ready.

She stepped toward the rocky outcropping where the two men waited.

Don shot up over from where he'd been pacing. "Well, well. Look who decided to show up."

"Did you come alone?" asked the second man.

Terror made it impossible for her to speak. She managed a nod. She glanced over at Ken. His eyes had grown wide—with fear or hope, she couldn't tell.

"Better check it out, Zeke," commanded Don.

The younger, redheaded man disappeared into the darkness of the trees. Clarissa tensed. If he found Ezra, they were all dead.

She cleared her throat and attempted to inject

some strength into her voice. "You need to let Ken go."

Don ambled toward her. "All in good time, sweetie." He leaned a little closer. "So did you decide that it wasn't worth it for all of your camping buddies to die because of you?"

His words cut right through her. She stood her ground and gave nothing away in her expression or her words. "I'm here. You need to untie Ken."

She could hear Zeke thrashing through the bushes and the trees. Her stomach somersaulted. Don's hand wavered over his gun. She counted the passing seconds and fought off a wave of nausea.

Zeke emerged from the trees. "She's telling the truth."

Don tilted his head toward Ken. "Untie the old guy."

"Sure, I'll do that." A look passed between Zeke and Don. A terror-filled chill ran down Clarissa's spine. Ken was not wearing a blindfold as Jan had been, and could recognize these thugs. They were going to shoot him as well as Clarissa.

She bided her time, unspoken prayers calming her nerves. Zeke pulled out a pocketknife. The blade glistened in the light. He set his gun on a rock and leaned over to cut Ken free.

Her heart pounded with anticipation. She had to choose the moment carefully. The window for escape was extremely narrow. She scanned the area around the camp. More than anything, she had to trust that Ezra was close enough to back her up.

Zeke finished cutting Ken free. Ken brought his hands to the front of his body. Now was the time to act, before Zeke reached for his gun.

"Now!" she screamed, barreling into Don, hitting him with all her weight. He stumbled backward, a stunned look on his face. Ezra appeared out of nowhere and disabled Zeke in a single motion.

Ken had already gotten to his feet when Don recovered enough to pull his gun. Ezra grabbed Clarissa's hand and pulled her into the trees, with Ken running ahead of them. The pop of Don's first pistol shot exploded in her ear.

As their feet pounded the soft undergrowth, the trees around her went by in a blur. The only sure thing she felt was the solidness of Ezra's grip on her hand as he pulled her through the forest.

Several more gunshots were fired behind them. Ken eventually slowed down and then lagged behind. Ezra led them on through the woods, never stopping to look at his surroundings or assess the direction they were going.

Out of breath, Clarissa finally let go of his hand, after twenty minutes of hard running. She leaned over and placed her hands on her knees, panting. "Don is not a runner," she gasped. "He won't be able to catch up with us."

Ezra peered from side to side. Clearly, he didn't want to stop moving, and he was barely out of breath. "What about the other guy?"

Clarissa shook her head.

Ken caught up with them. He struggled for air, pressing his hand to his heart. "My wife, is she okay?"

Clarissa nodded. "She and Bruce are headed toward the lodge. We're going to meet up with them."

Ezra focused on the forest behind them. "We can't wait here much longer."

Zeke catching up with them was a strong possibility, but Clarissa was too exhausted to run any farther. "Let us catch our breath." She cupped her hand on Ken's shoulder, whose face was red from exertion.

"We have to keep moving. The path reconnects with the main trail soon." Ezra took off at a slower pace, looking back at them over his shoulder.

She tugged on Ken's sleeve. "He's right. We'd better get moving." Clarissa glanced behind her before following, with Ken on her heels.

Though Ezra had slowed to a brisk walk, he kept moving.

Once they reconnected with the main trail, Clarissa anticipated catching up with Jan and Bruce. But as the sun got lower in the sky, that hope faded. Maybe they had been able to move fast enough to arrive at the lodge already.

She and Ezra hadn't eaten anything since the rabbit they'd had for breakfast. It might have been even longer for Ken.

Clarissa stopped on the trail, turned and waited for Ken to catch up. Fatigue and hunger threatened to overtake her, but she knew it would be a waste of breath to ask Ezra to stop. A sense of urgency dogged their every step. They had to find Bruce and Jan.

Clarissa looked at the sky. Off in the distance a helicopter hovered, and then banked and gained altitude. The chopper wasn't anywhere near them. It certainly wasn't close enough for them to build a signal fire and hope to be rescued.

Once Ken had caught up, she trudged ahead until she walked beside Ezra.

"How far away is the lodge?"

"In broad daylight on a full belly, we'd be close. But at the pace we're going I'd say an hour or more." He looked over his shoulder. "How is Ken doing?"

"He's hanging in there. I think the hope of being reunited with Jan again is motivating him."

"Those two have been married a long time. You don't break a bond like that easily."

They continued for a while longer. Ezra stopped suddenly. His arm shot out in front of her, indicating that she needed to be still. Ken caught up to them.

Clarissa couldn't hear or see anything amiss. The helicopter was long gone. Gradually, she became aware of her own heavy inhale and exhale and the rapid beating of her heart.

A moment later, Ezra seemed satisfied that he hadn't heard anything.

His brisk walk turned into a jog. Clarissa forced herself to keep pace with him, focusing on the path in front of her. The trail curved gradually upward. At the top of the ridgeline, Ezra stopped to catch his breath. "Not far now. And it's all downhill from here."

Clarissa looked down the sparsely forested slope, but saw no lights or structure that would indicate a lodge was just ahead of them. They made their way down the hill.

They'd managed to evade the two thugs for now. Clarissa wondered what kind of resources Max would call upon to make sure she didn't get out of this forest alive. Did Don and Zeke have a way of communicating with him? Was that helicopter somehow connected to Max?

The roof of the lodge came into view. She looked out again, expecting to see lights. If the lodge was still dark, had Jan and Bruce even made it? Certainly, they would have encountered them on the trail…unless something had scared them off and away from the lodge completely.

NINE

Ezra grew warier as they approached the lodge. He slowed to a walk, looking for any sign of life even as a sense of impending doom set in.

Please, God, let them be safe.

Clarissa and Ken caught up to him. He cleared his mind of anything that spoke of disaster. *Focus on the here and now. You can't change past choices.*

The outline of the lodge became clearer, a large log cabin with a porch. They were coming in from the side.

"Is there somebody there, like a caretaker?" Clarissa came up beside him.

"Somebody does come up when there is a long interval without guests. But he wouldn't be here now," Ezra said.

Their feet crunched on the dry evergreen needles as they swung around to the front of the house. Ezra was the first up the steps. He pushed the door open. Clarissa pressed in close behind him.

The room was completely dark. "Hello?" He stepped inside.

"Jan? Bruce?" Clarissa's voice was filled with anxiety.

Floorboards creaked somewhere in the lodge. She gasped and pressed a little closer to Ezra.

Ken's voice sounded behind them, speaking in a hushed tone. "Do you suppose that's...?"

Ezra didn't want to build up hope, only to have it be dashed. "Sometimes the raccoons get in."

He moved through the great room, touching a wall to orient himself in the dark.

"Jan, are you here?" Ken's voice had become a bit more forceful.

The silence that followed embedded doubt in Ezra's mind. What had happened to them? He questioned the choices he'd made as a leader.

They moved through the dark, industrial-sized kitchen. Stainless-steel appliances and countertops shone in the darkness. A glow barely evident in the small window in the door caught his attention. He hurried across the floor and swung the door open to the backyard.

Outside, a small fire had been built. Bruce emerged from the trees holding a bundle of wood in his good arm.

Ken swept past Ezra down the stairs. "Where is Jan?"

Bruce pointed to the forest behind him. "Getting more firewood."

Ezra patted Bruce's shoulder. "You made it." He gestured to the fire.

"We couldn't get anything to work in the lodge," said Bruce.

"The generator must be down," Ezra said.

"We were hungry and there are lots of canned goods in there. So we decided to cook over the fire like you taught us."

Ken emerged from the forest, his arms wrapped around his weary but elated wife.

Clarissa touched her stomach. "I haven't eaten since this morning."

Bruce glowed with pride. "We've got lots of food."

"I'll go have a look at that generator," Ezra stated. Guilt ate at his inside as he made his way to the generator in the utility room. These people had been through way more than they'd bargained for, yet a simple meal seemed to make them happy. Within minutes, he found the gasoline for the generator, and it sputtered to life. Lights came on in the lodge, and he heard a cry of exultation from the group outside. He shook his head. The cheerful noise lifted his own spirits. What an amazing bunch of people.

He returned to where the four of them had gathered around the fire.

Bruce held out a plate to him. "Got some grub for you."

Ezra took the plate. Though his stomach growled, his mind raced with everything that needed to be done to guarantee they got out of here safely. Still, he knew he'd work better on a full stomach. He took several bites of the stew Bruce had prepared.

He could feel the eyes of the others on him as they waited for explanations and instructions. If everything went right, a rescue helicopter would be on the way once he radioed for help. "Bruce, I think you have a future as a camp cook," he declared.

Bruce glowed from the compliment. "I just did what you taught us. Use the resources that are available."

Ezra took a few more bites. Jan and Ken had settled on the steps by the kitchen door, and Clarissa sat close to the fire on a log. "I'm going to radio for a helicopter. In the meantime, you should be able to find more food, plus a fully stocked first aid kit to fix whatever scratches and bruises you have. With the generator out for so long, there won't be any hot water, but you might be able to manage a lukewarm shower."

"How long before the helicopter can get here?" Ken wrapped his arm around his wife.

"Six to eight hours." Ezra's heart sank as he thought about Leonard. They'd have to send a search party out to find him.

Ezra could feel a weight drop on him. "I owe you people an apology. This was not what you signed up for." His throat grew tight. "You are the most impressive group of people I've ever worked with."

Bruce stood close to the fire, the flames dancing on his pale skin. "Survival isn't about a planned itinerary. Guess we just got some real-world experience."

"Who are those men who are after Clarissa?" Ken asked.

She lifted her head, her glance darting around to each person. "It's a long story."

"It's one I deserve to hear." Ken narrowed his gaze at her, his anger evident. The trauma of the past twenty-four hours had clearly caught up with him.

Jan placed a hand on his shoulder. "I'm just glad we're all here and help will soon be on the way."

"What about Leonard? Where is Leonard?" Ken scooted away from his wife.

"We were unable to find him." Ezra looked

at the ground. "What we hope is that he made his way back down the mountain."

"What we *hope?*" said Ken, his voice full of accusation.

"Ken, I understand your anger and I don't blame you," Ezra said.

Bruce stepped in. "Ezra and Clarissa pulled me out of a freezing river. They saved my life. I'd say Ezra has done the best he could, considering what happened."

Ken shot to his feet, his gaze filled with challenge.

"That storm came out of nowhere, honey," Jan soothed.

Ken whirled around to face Clarissa. "Yeah, but those men didn't."

Clarissa rose to her feet and stepped toward him. Her voice, though soft, maintained a tone of strength. "Those men are my doing."

"Who are they, Clarissa? Why are they after you?" Jan stepped closer to Clarissa. Her voice didn't hold the condemnation that Ken's had.

Ezra listened as Clarissa explained everything she knew about the men. Though she fingered the cuffs of her shirt nervously, she spoke with a clear voice, despite how hard this must be for her. What a brave woman she was.

The others were silent when she finished. Jan

spoke first. "Well, I, for one, am going to get cleaned up."

"I'll go radio for help," Ezra said. "It might be a good idea if all of us went inside." The two men were out there somewhere. They might know about the lodge and they might not. Either way, it wasn't wise to stay out in the open.

"I'll put the fire out," Bruce offered.

Ezra was aware of Ken's stern glare as he passed him. Once everyone was inside, Ezra checked all the doors to make sure they were locked, and then he latched the windows. He was in the great room closing a window when Clarissa found him.

"You're thinking they might come here, aren't you?" Her mouth tightened, revealing the stress she was under.

"We can only speculate about what those men will do, or how much they know about where we were headed. What we have to do is take precautions. The helicopter won't get here for some time."

His statement did nothing to erase the worry from her face. He stepped toward her and touched her cheek lightly. Did he see yearning in those wide blue eyes? For what? He remembered his impulsive kiss. He'd meant what he'd said. He did care about her.

He pulled his hand away. In another time and

another place, perhaps he'd pursue those feelings to see where they led. But this wasn't the right moment. He needed to get some help up to the lodge and get these people home safe.

Clarissa stepped back, as well.

Ezra went to the office, where the radio was. He keyed the device, but heard no sound. After fiddling with the controls for several minutes, he dropped his face in his hands. The radio wasn't working.

As she took a quick cold shower, Clarissa was well aware of how precarious their situation was. Anything could happen in the six to eight hours it would take for the helicopter to get up here. She slipped into the change of clothes she'd brought with her.

She looked at herself in the mirror as she combed out her hair. Fear gripped her heart. The prospect of going back to Discovery was not a happy one. Max would be waiting for her.

She couldn't stay here at the lodge. She couldn't continue on by herself. If only she could figure out why Max was so bent on wiping her from the face of the earth.

To go to all this trouble, Max had to be engaged in some sort of criminal activity. Clarissa must have seen some trace of it, something that he believed she could use against him. She thought about every document that had come across her desk. The computer files she'd had access to. The properties Max owned. None of it set off any alarms.

She heard a light rapping at the door. When she opened it, Jan stood there, looking cleaned up from her own shower. With the mud and dirt no longer a factor, Clarissa could see the gashes on Jan's face and arms. What had those men put her through?

Clarissa reached up to touch the scratch on Jan's forehead. "I'm so sorry about that." Her throat went tight.

"I can't say I'm not upset. But that's not what I came here to talk to you about. I wanted to apologize for Ken."

"I understand why he's so mad," Clarissa said.

"He gets angry when he can't control things," Jan told her. "Before all this happened, we were both talking about how much we liked you. We never had any children." Jan's eyes filled with tears. "I always thought if we had a daughter, she would be like you."

Clarissa let the words sink in. Then she wrapped her arms around the older woman's neck and hugged her for a long moment.

When they finally stepped back, Jan touched Clarissa's cheek lightly. "Ken will come around.

He will." She shrugged. "I guess we're supposed to try to get some sleep before the helicopter comes."

"The rooms must be upstairs. I didn't notice any down here."

"I feel like I could sleep for a hundred years." Jan retreated down the hallway.

After pulling her hair up in a ponytail, Clarissa thought she'd find Ezra in the office, waiting for any additional radio calls. But the room was empty. She wandered into the great room, where someone had built a fledgling fire.

To feed the flames, she began balling up some of the newspaper stacked beside the fireplace. She'd put several pages in the glowing embers when one of the news stories caught her eye. The paper was local, from a few days ago, probably brought up here by the last hikers that had used the lodge.

Clarissa held the paper closer to see better in the dim light. The headline read Woman Found Dead in Car. A woman's body had been found in a car with Wyoming plates. Cause of death was still to be determined.

Clarissa studied the photograph of the car taken from a distance. She took in a sharp breath as she kept reading. The woman was identified as Sondra Nelson.

She leaped to her feet. This had to be connected to Max. Tension coiled around her neck and twisted the muscles in her back. She covered her mouth with her hand to keep from crying out.

What did it mean? What did it all mean?

The lodge was completely silent. She pushed down the rising panic, only to have a wave of sorrow wash over her. Memories of Sondra's kindness to her, of the two of them laughing together, flooded through her mind. How could this be happening?

Ezra burst through the front door. "The antenna for the radio is down. I could use your help trying to get it back up."

Still reeling from the reality of Sondra's death, Clarissa followed him outside and across the grounds to a long garage where he had propped a ladder against the roof.

He headed up the ladder. "I've got the tools up there already. I need someone to hold the antenna so I can try to anchor it back in place."

She climbed up after him.

"Here, hold this bracket right here." He grabbed a screwdriver from the toolbox. "This thing was blown clean off the roof. I had to drag it out of the trees. I hope this fixes it."

Clarissa could hear the tension in his voice. "What if we can't radio for help?"

He stopped twisting the screwdriver. "We'll

figure this out. Maybe one of the others knows more about radios than I do. Where is everybody anyway?"

"I think they're resting or getting cleaned up." The shock of Sondra's death and now this setback was almost too much. "What if this doesn't work?"

He paused and looked directly at her. "We're not there yet. Deal with the now, not the what-ifs."

Ezra's ability to focus in a crisis buoyed her up.

He rifled through the toolbox. "You know, Clarissa, when we get back to town I'll go with you to the police. I don't know why you didn't do that in the first place."

She knew Ezra was talking about when they got back to encourage her to believe that that would happen. "I'm sure all your encounters with the police have been positive, but mine haven't," she told him.

"Oh?" He was focused on screwing another bracket in place and wasn't looking in her direction. That made it easier for her to say the next words.

"When I was a little girl, there were times when my father's drinking got bad enough for the neighbors to call the police. I remember holding on to this stuffed animal I had, and standing in the hallway, when the police officer showed up, asking my father to explain why he'd been so loud. I remember being four or five and longing for that policeman to take me out of that house." Pain pierced through her as the vividness of the memory came back. "But he never did."

Ezra stopped what he was doing and sat back. He shook his head, his voice filled with compassion. "I had no idea." He scooted toward her, taking her hand in his. "We will see to it that Max gets what's coming to him."

"I don't see how. I don't know why he's after me, and I can't prove anything. I can't even prove that Max sent Don and that other guy." Sondra's death was still foremost in Clarissa's mind, but she didn't want to burden Ezra any more than he already was.

"We'll figure it out," he said, shaking the antenna to see if it was going to stay in place.

We? She wasn't accustomed to that pronoun. "You say that with so much confidence. Max told the police in L.A. lies about me and they believed him."

"I know some of the police officers in this town. They won't fall for that kind of thing." He rested his palm on her cheek. "It's going to be okay."

She relished the warmth of his touch. As she

looked into his brown eyes, she wanted to believe him, to trust him. She pulled away, fearing that he would kiss her again. She wasn't sure what the first kiss had even meant.

He scooted away, as well, and moved toward the ladder. "I've got to go see if that fixed it."

From the roof, Clarissa watched him walk toward the lodge, only to turn suddenly and head into the forest. What had he seen?

TEN

Ezra turned abruptly when he saw the light bobbing in the distance through the trees. He hurried to head off whatever threat was coming toward the lodge, and the people he needed to keep safe.

He ran toward where he'd seen the light, slowing as he drew closer. It didn't matter that he didn't have a gun. If he didn't give them time to draw on him, then he was certain he could handle the two armed thugs. Judging from their earlier encounter, they had minimum training and relied mostly on their brawn and firepower.

Ezra wove through the trees, looking and listening for signs of the men. He saw only one light some distance away, appearing and disappearing in the thick forest. It was a flame, not a flashlight. At least one of the men had made a torch. He searched for a second light but saw nothing. Clarissa had thought that the bigger of the two thugs might not be up for a long-distance hike. Maybe only the younger one had made it this far?

Ezra eased toward where he'd seen the light until the sound of pounding footsteps filled the night. He stopped behind a tree and waited, shutting out extraneous noise and focusing on the uneven footfalls until he knew the man was close. Ezra leaped toward him, wrapping an arm around the man's neck and twisting, causing the man to fall to the ground.

Ezra reached for the torch before anything caught on fire. He shone it on the man, who shaded his eyes from the light. "Well, now, that's a nice how do you do!"

"Leonard?" Ezra bent forward as joy surged through him. He reached his hand out to the older man, pulled him to his feet and embraced him. He couldn't contain his happiness. "How did you get here?"

"You did leave us with a compass and you did tell us where the lodge was. I was closer to here than to the bottom of the mountain. Even if I'd wanted to hike out there, I wasn't sure if I'd be able to break into that van and get the engine started."

Ezra continued to shake his head. "I'm so sorry. We looked for you."

"I got all turned around when I went looking

for Bruce and that storm came in. Found the camp after you guys must have left."

"We had to keep moving. So much has happened. We need to get back to the lodge so I can radio for help. You must be hungry. I'll fill you in while you eat."

"Sounds good to me." Leonard pulled the pistol out of his waistband. "I did manage to kill some meat."

"I didn't know you were carrying that."

"I'm a retired detective. I always carry a gun." Leonard pulled a phone out of his pocket. "The gun isn't my only cheat. I took this, hoping to get a signal. I've got a grandbaby on the way."

"I'm actually glad you have that gun," said Ezra. "And if you can get any kind of signal, then the phone will be useful, too."

They were working their way through the forest toward the lodge when the whirring sound of helicopter blades reverberated in the distance.

Ezra tilted his head and tensed as the chopper drew closer. Since he hadn't been able to call for help, he wondered who was inside—friend or foe?

From the yard where she'd been looking for Ezra, Clarissa saw the blinking lights of the helicopter before she heard it. It went down some distance from the lodge, where there must be a landing pad.

She ran through the forest, pushing branches out of the way, but then slowed as she drew nearer to where the craft had landed. The slicing whir of the blades stopped before she came into the clearing. She could hear men's voices. This could be unexpected help...or something much more dangerous.

She headed toward the helicopter as one man got out. As she drew closer, she got a clearer view of another one sitting next to the pilot. She stopped in her tracks.

Max.

Momentarily paralyzed by terror, Clarissa watched as Max pushed himself out of the helicopter. Then two other men got out, ones she didn't recognize. She stepped back into the shadows, uncertain if Max had seen her or not. Spinning around, she sprinted through the forest, running so wildly she lost all sense of direction.

She could hear the men coming after her. Max's commanding voice was distinct from the others. Clarissa ran, not in the direction that would lead her back to the lodge, but away from it. It was her they wanted. Maybe she couldn't save herself, but she could save the others.

All the trees looked the same to her. She kept running, not sure where she'd end up.

A hand grabbed her from behind. She swung around, ready to fight. Ezra's familiar face gazed down at her, and he caught her wrist before she could land a blow.

"Where are you going?"

"It's Max and more of his henchmen." Fear froze her words in her throat. She could barely speak. Her heart pounded erratically against her rib cage.

He grabbed her hand and ran. The lodge came into view.

"But the others," she screamed, trying to pull him in a different direction.

Ezra held her hand tighter and kept running. She could hear the sound of the men behind her. They'd come into the clearing. The lodge was still forty yards away. A pistol shot sliced the air by her shoulder. Ezra pulled her to the ground.

She could see Jan through the window. The older woman came out on the porch. Ezra signaled for her to get back inside. Grabbing Clarissa at the waist, he pulled her to her feet. With the strength of his arms bearing her up, they stumbled toward the door of the lodge.

He locked the door behind them and pulled the shades over the windows. The others had come down the stairs. Clarissa registered shock when she saw Leonard.

Ken stepped forward, wrapping his arms around Jan and pulling her close. "They're back, aren't they?" Despite his attempt at bravado, the trembling in Ken's voice gave away his fear.

Ezra hesitated when he glanced at Ken, as though trying to formulate a plan. "There is a pantry off the kitchen that has no windows and a door that locks from the inside. I want you to take Jan there." He glanced around. "Where's Bruce?"

"Resting upstairs," Jan answered. "He doesn't feel so good."

Desperation clouded Clarissa's thoughts. How were they going to get Bruce the medical attention he needed? "I should leave here. I can lead them away. That will give you time to get the radio working and call in some help." She moved toward the door.

Ezra grabbed her arm. "Clarissa, I'm not turning you into bait again."

Jan stepped forward. "I agree with Ezra. That's too dangerous for you."

They had seconds to decide what to do. Max's men were closing in.

Leonard stepped forward. "I've got thirty years police experience under my belt, and I know a little bit about radios." He pulled the gun out of his waistband. "I say Ezra goes with Clarissa. I can take care of the others and make sure we get out of here safely."

She read the turmoil in Ezra's expression. He felt an obligation to everyone present.

"What if they take us hostage for her again?" Ken asked.

"It won't come to that," said Leonard. He cupped his hand on Ezra's shoulder. "I won't let it come to that."

Ezra nodded slowly. "We'll go out the front door. Make sure they see us. If they don't take the bait, we'll come back and deal with them together."

Leonard turned toward Ken. "Get Bruce and your wife to that pantry."

Clarissa grabbed her pack where she'd left it by the couch, while Ezra stepped to the door. He pulled the curtain aside and peered out the window. "I don't see them yet."

All the others except for Leonard left the great room.

"This is the right thing to do," she said. At least this way the others had a fighting chance.

"It's the best choice when there are no good choices." He peered back through the window. "I saw movement in the trees." He unlatched the door and then shouted, "Leonard, lock this behind us." Ezra checked the window one more time and then reached for Clarissa's hand. He pulled her through the doorway, across the porch and down the steps just as the men emerged from the woods.

One of the men raised his gun right away. The shot hit a post on the porch as Clarissa and Ezra swung around the side of the lodge, running toward the long, narrow garage where the antenna was mounted. Ezra led her inside the building where several ATVs were stored. Everything in the garage was covered in a layer of dust. He pushed a tall tool chest against the door.

The men banged on the door barely a moment later and pushed against it.

"Let's hope these still have gas in them." Ezra started an ATV while Clarissa opened the rear door. She had just climbed on the back of the four-wheeler when one man broke down the front door.

Ezra roared through the open back door as the closest thug approached, pulling his gun from his waistband. The garage opened up to rolling hills, which didn't provide much cover. Clarissa looked over her shoulder. The man was aiming his gun.

"Duck!" Ezra leaned down over the handlebars and Clarissa bent forward, as well. He turned the ATV sharply. The shot hit somewhere to the side of her.

When she looked over her shoulder again, the second man had come out on an ATV and the first had disappeared. Hopefully, to get another ATV, not to go back to the lodge. Right before Ezra steered around a corner, Max came around the side of the shed. He stood at the top of the hill, arms crossed.

The picture of him branded Clarissa's consciousness and sent a chill over her skin. She turned her head away and held on tighter to Ezra.

Shifting into the highest gear, Ezra pushed the ATV as hard as he dared over the rough terrain. He could hear the other four-wheeler behind him. Clarissa pressed close to him and held on tight. The rolling hills intersected with a narrow dirt road, and Ezra increased his speed. Gradually, the mechanical hum of the other ATV faded.

"Can you see him?"

Clarissa shifted on the seat behind him. "No." Maybe their pursuer's ATV had fallen over, which they were prone to do. Or maybe he'd run out of gas. Ezra's own gas gauge was dangerously low. They'd be on foot soon enough.

In the distance, they heard the helicopter lifting off, the whirring of the blades growing more intense as the chopper approached. Ezra stood up on the ATV, trying to gain speed and control when they went downhill. The engine sputtered. The gas gauge was on empty.

"Come on," he coaxed. "Just a little farther."

At the bottom of the road, the ATV quit altogether. Clarissa leaped off first, turning in a half circle to take in her surroundings. As quick-thinking as she was, she was probably formulating some sort of escape plan.

Ezra checked the storage area under the seat of the ATV. He grabbed the length of rope he found there and stuffed it in Clarissa's backpack, grateful that she had thought to grab it.

She gazed at him, her eyes filled with questions. To go back the way they'd come would be suicide. Depending on where Don and Zeke were, Max had at least four men and a pilot helping him. They must be communicating with each other. Where could he and Clarissa find safety?

Engine noises, distinct but faraway, permeated the forest. The ATV rider must have fixed whatever trouble he'd encountered. The helicopter grew louder, as well.

"Tree cover." Ezra took her hand and headed toward the thicker part of the forest. They ran without stopping, the whirring of the chopper blades indicating that their aerial pursuer was still too close for comfort.

They slipped into the thick forest. As she sprinted ahead of him, Clarissa stumbled. Ezra caught her before she could hit the forest floor, holding her around the waist. Both of them were out of breath. He backed up to a tree, still clutching her close.

The noise of the helicopter faded. He waited for his own breathing to slow so he could listen for the ATV. He was aware of his arm around Clarissa's waist, her palm pressed against his chest. She smelled faintly of flowers. His heart skipped a beat when he looked down at her. Was that trust he saw in her eyes?

"Do you think we lost them?" she whispered.

She didn't pull free of his embrace. "I'm not sure. Wait awhile longer," he said.

The minutes passed, with no sound to indicate they were still a target. Clarissa's proximity made Ezra's skin tingle, and his heart beat faster. Her mouth was full and inviting. He wanted to kiss her.

He dropped his arm from around her waist and stepped back. The first kiss had been impulsive, born of his need to convince her she mattered. He had stepped over a line. He didn't know her whole story, but he knew enough to see that people had let her down when she needed them. As much as he wanted to kiss her, as wonderful as she felt in his arms, he didn't want to do anything to destroy the fragile trust he saw in her eyes.

And he sure didn't want to revisit the pain his former fiancée had caused him.

She craned her neck from side to side. "I don't hear anything."

"Me, either." He shook his head, doubting that they could have thrown their pursuers off that easily. They were probably regrouping and coming up with a new battle plan.

"What do we do now?"

"It makes more sense to head over the mountain than to go back the way we came," he said.

"You mean we'll head toward that little town you talked about instead of back to Discovery?"

"We're closer to it at this point. I don't want to risk leading them back to the lodge, and we know they're probably waiting for us to come that way and head toward the van."

She nodded. "They won't be expecting us to go the opposite way."

"When the others are able to radio for help, they'll explain what happened. The authorities will send out rescue teams."

The furrow between Clarissa's eyebrows

deepened, indicating her level of anxiety. "*If* they get the radio working."

"They're going to make it," he said.

She crossed her arms over her chest. "What about us? Have you hiked over that mountain before?"

He saw the fear in her eyes. "A couple dozen times. I take advanced groups up there."

"I don't know anything about mountain climbing."

The breeze ruffled her soft blond hair and again he was struck by how fragile she looked, an appearance that belied the core of iron beneath. He stepped toward her, brushing her cheek with his knuckles. "From what I've seen, you can handle it just fine."

Her full lips curved up in a faint smile. "I hope you're right."

"Okay, let's get going." He turned to go.

"Ezra?"

He swung back around to face her. "Yes?"

"Why are you doing this? Why are you helping me?"

His commitment had gone beyond just a sense of responsibility to a client. He felt something much deeper for Clarissa. He couldn't bring himself to say that, though, afraid of how she might react. "Because you deserve better than having some murderous jerk chase you through the woods. You deserve a shot at a normal life."

Her face glowed with affection and gratitude as she whispered a thank-you.

Her soft words warmed his heart. "Let's get moving." He pivoted and pushed through the trees.

They walked until they came to a shallow stream.

"You still have your canteen with you?"

She slipped the pack off and searched until she found both the canteen and the water purifier. "There's no more food left in here."

"I can take care of that. Why don't you fill up the canteen? I need to orient myself and figure how far we are from the trailhead."

He slipped around a bend in the creek to determine where they were on the mountain. His last image of Clarissa before he stepped out of view was of her bending over the creek, dipping the canteen in the water. The evening light played on her creamy skin and brought out the gold in her hair.

He'd wandered about a hundred yards into the forest when instinct told him it was a mistake to leave Clarissa alone even for a few minutes.

ELEVEN

Wind, birds, the creaking of the branches—all the sounds of the forest calmed Clarissa as the cool creek water flowed over her hands. She knew she couldn't ever totally let her guard down. Max and his hired thugs would figure out which way they'd gone soon enough. For a brief moment, though, she could stop and catch her breath.

She straightened up, wiped her forehead and twisted the cap on the canteen. She couldn't comprehend why Ezra was so willing to stay with her, to endure all this, or why the others had, for the most part, been willing to forgive her.

She heard a noise and glanced up. Across the creek, one of Max's thugs stood leering down at her. He was a square-jawed man with big teeth. "I knew you'd need water sooner or later."

Terror slammed against her with the force of a truck. She wheezed in air as she scrambled to her feet.

He splashed through the shallow stream and grabbed her, yanking her toward him. He pressed his face close to hers. "Did you think I'd give up that easily? I've been moving up and down this river for the past hour."

She struggled to get away. He tightened his grip on her.

Though fear nearly made her knees buckle, Clarissa narrowed her eyes at her assailant. "What are you going to do?" She spoke through clenched teeth to hide how afraid she was.

"I think you know." His gruff voice pelted her.

She softened her expression, allowing him to see some of her fear. The tactic made him loosen his grip on her as a sneer of delight formed on his face.

Taking advantage of his distraction, she kicked him hard in the shin. When he let go of her, she whirled away and tried to dart toward the forest, but he grabbed her shirt collar and pulled her back. She tried to angle away.

The man turned slightly, as though he'd heard something, and then he crumpled to the ground. Ezra stood facing her as the man lay gasping for air. Ezra landed another blow. The thug stopped moving.

"You'll have to show me how to do that sometime." She tried to sound normal, but her voice gave away how the assault had shaken her.

Ezra pulled her into a quick hug, holding her close. If only she could stay in the safety of his arms! But the man on the ground started to stir.

Ezra released her, then brushed her cheek lightly. "We've gotta go."

She nodded.

He scooped the canteen and backpack off the ground, glancing up and down the stream. "Did you see his four-wheeler anywhere?"

She shook her head. "He said he'd been walking up and down the river looking for us."

"Maybe we'll get lucky, huh?" Ezra fastened on her backpack. "You go in front of me."

The man on the ground moaned and rolled over on his side.

They ran through the night until it grew completely dark. Finally, Ezra stopped, dumping the backpack on the ground. "I'll go find us some dinner. Build a fire, but keep it small. We don't want to give away our position."

Clarissa gathered kindling and pulled the matches from her pack. Ezra would probably consider this cheating when it came to building a fire. She smiled at the idea. The days when their survival had been only a lesson seemed like a million miles away. She kept the fire low, warming her hands over the flames.

Ezra returned with an animal already skinned and on a stick. "Squirrel."

"I won't complain."

"Just pretend it's a steak dinner," he said.

"I'm not that fond of steak. I'll pretend it's fettuccine with Alfredo sauce."

"That's kind of a stretch," he said.

She appreciated the banter. They ate a meal of squirrel and water. The meat was sinewy but tasty. As empty as her stomach was, anything would have tasted good.

Ezra took the last few bites of his meat and tossed the bones toward the fire. "We can only rest for a few hours. Night is our best time to keep moving."

Clarissa was unbelievably tired. Her legs hurt from all the running they'd been doing. But Ezra wasn't complaining, so she wouldn't, either.

"I'm going to have to put the fire out. We can't risk being spotted," he said. He rose to his feet and kicked dirt on the fire until even the glowing embers disappeared. The night felt instantly colder. She crossed her arms over her body.

Ezra sat down beside her. "There should be a space blanket in your pack." He rifled through it until he recovered a tiny packet. He opened it and pulled out what looked like a giant piece of thin tinfoil. He draped it over her shoulders.

She stared up at the stars. "Do you suppose the others were able to get the radio to work?"

Ezra's answer was slow in coming. "Hard to say. I haven't seen any other helicopter in the sky besides Max's."

Pain stabbed through her. "I just wish we could know for sure that they're safe. After all they've been through, if Max did anything to them..." Anger stopped the words in her throat.

"I think our strategy worked." Ezra looked off into the distance. "Clarissa, I have to ask again—do you still not know why this man is after you?"

She rested her face in her hands. "I don't know. I keep trying to piece it together. It has to be connected to my work with him. He must think I know something or saw something."

"Did you?"

"Not that I can recall. Nothing that was clearly illegal." Her mind functioned like a camera, reviewing everything that she had done as his assistant. "There were some things with the bookkeeping that were off. Money would be deposited for the sale of a house, but then paperwork for the sale would come in a long time after the deposit."

"Anything else that you remember?"

She pulled the blanket tighter as the evening chill settled around her. "It's just all these jumbled pieces. My friend Sondra was supposed to pick me up in Discovery." Clarissa's throat tightened. "She used to work for Max, too. She never showed—that's why I joined your class."

Clarissa placed her hand over her heart as tears welled in her eyes. "I saw a newspaper at the lodge. She was found dead just outside of town...." Clarissa couldn't hold back the tears any longer. The days of trauma and everything that had taken place overwhelmed her. She covered her face with her hands and sobbed.

Ezra's hand gently touched her back. "So much of a burden for one person to carry alone."

She turned to face him. Compassion shone in his eyes. She leaned toward him, and he enveloped her in his arms. Her cheek brushed against the softness of his flannel shirt. He smelled faintly of soap and evergreens. Her crying subsided.

She moved to pull away, but he held her tighter. "Stay," he said. "We'll both be warmer, and you can get some sleep."

His holding her felt awkward at first, but gradually she relaxed in his embrace.

How long had it been since she'd been held by a man? Ten years. After the father of her baby had walked away, her heart had turned to stone.

She'd made a vow never to let anyone in again. As she rested her cheek against Ezra's shoulder, she felt that hardness being chipped away.

"You know, Clarissa, you could have shared some of this with me right away. You don't have to go through everything alone."

"Guess it's just a habit. My father died when I was five. I've been taking care of myself ever since."

"That's just not right." She caught the tremble of emotion in Ezra's voice.

The fatigue from the day and all the running they had done weighted her muscles. Her eyelids grew heavy. She fell asleep to the steady rhythm of Ezra's breathing, feeling warm and safe despite the uncertainty that loomed over their lives.

Ezra leaned back against the tree and closed his eyes. He slept lightly, waking often to evaluate if any threat was close. Any out-of-place noise or a light even in the distance would mean they'd have to run. The man they'd disabled by the river had probably figured out where they were going. He would tell the others.

Clarissa slept comfortably in Ezra's arms. She'd stiffened when he had first wrapped his arm around her. He hadn't meant to make her uncomfortable. His invitation had been purely practical. They needed to stay warm. But now as he held her, he liked feeling the softness of her hair on his chin and the way she smelled like the air after a spring rain.

Even with the flow of good feelings, he had to remind himself that Clarissa was nothing like Emma. Not every woman would hurt him like she had. He wanted to believe that.

He still felt a sense of indignation about what Clarissa had shared with him. She had been without a family since she was five. He could only imagine what she had been through. She deserved so much better, deserved a chance at a happy life.

He dozed for a while, but awoke to a droning sound in the distance. He couldn't see the lights of the helicopter, but he could hear it.

He sat up straighter. "Clarissa, wake up."

"Hmm?" She still wasn't coherent.

He pulled away from her and pushed himself to his feet. "They're around here. I can hear them."

"I don't hear anything." Her voice was still a little groggy, but she rose to her feet and stuffed the space blanket in the backpack. "What did you hear?"

"Listen," he whispered.

She leaned against him, not moving or talking. A gasp escaped her lips as she noticed the sound of the helicopter blades. "How far away do you think it is?"

Why couldn't he see the chopper yet? It must be behind the trees or the rock formation to the west. "Sounds like it's some distance off." He couldn't discern what direction the sound was coming from. "We've got time, but we'd better get moving." He put the backpack on and started walking. There wasn't a huge amount of trees this close to the rock formation, so they'd need the cover of darkness to hide them. It was a good thing he could get around at night in these woods just as easily as if it were daytime. He headed in the general direction of the mountain, glancing over his shoulder to make sure Clarissa was keeping up.

The mechanical chopper noise became more oppressive, and the lights of the chopper came into view, changing elevation and directions as it searched for them. In this open field, they'd be too easy to spot. They needed to get to the cover of the trees before they were seen.

"Hurry." He reached back and grabbed Clarissa's hand as he increased their pace. They were both in dark clothes and not using flashlights. The helicopter would almost have to be on top of them before they would be noticed.

The forest seemed to move farther away the

harder they ran. If they could get into the trees, they wouldn't be spotted at all.

The chopper veered toward them suddenly, catching them in the bright headlights. The wind created from the rotation of the blades swirled around them. The trees were still a hundred yards away.

Ezra could make out the silhouette of a man in the open door to the chopper as it whirled around and hovered. He barely heard the first rifle shot above the clang of the engines as he wrapped his arm around Clarissa and pulled her to the ground.

The second rifle shot tore through the backpack. Ezra heard the ting of metal being hit, probably the canteen absorbing the bullet. Cold water soaking the back of his shirt confirmed his theory.

They crawled wounded-soldier style toward a ditch. The helicopter gained elevation and turned, trying to maneuver to get a better angle on them. Ezra grabbed Clarissa's shirt. "Run as fast as you can. Hit the ground when you need to."

"Aren't you coming with me?"

"Two targets are harder to hit than one. I'll catch up with you in the trees."

She hesitated. The helicopter descended and started to move in.

"We don't have time to discuss this," he said. "Stay low. I'll run out first so they'll go after me."

He veered away from her and pushed himself to his feet. Hopefully, the chopper would target him, and she'd have a chance to get to the forest.

From the corner of his eye, he watched as Clarissa ran fifty feet and dived to the ground. He did the same. As the helicopter loomed closer, the clanging engine noises and whirring of the blades pressed in around him. He couldn't see Clarissa anymore. Up ahead, the trees seemed to be a million miles away. The chopper sounded as if it was right on top of him. He burst to his feet and ran a short distance.

The rifleman got off a shot that came dangerously close to hitting him. Ezra zigzagged as the edge of the forest drew ever closer. A shot sounded some distance from him. If he could stay out of the lights of the chopper, he might make it.

He still couldn't spot Clarissa. He hoped it hadn't been a mistake to split up. He was within twenty feet of the trees now. He willed his legs to pump harder. The helicopter rose up behind him. As he stepped into the cover of the woods, the chopper gained more altitude. He ran toward the thicker trees. Though he could still hear the helicopter, it grew fainter. The pilot was circling around the forest, waiting for him to come out, or the tree cover to thin enough to get a shot.

Ezra turned his attention to finding Clarissa. He darted from tree to tree, moving in the general direction of where she might have entered the forest. He called her name, feeling a rising sense of panic when she didn't answer.

Though his visibility was limited in the darkness, he didn't dare turn the flashlight on. The chopper was still hovering above him. He searched the trees, shrouded in shadow, and called her name one more time as he ran.

After about five minutes, he stopped, hoping to hear her voice. The noise of the helicopter had ended. He feared the thugs had touched down and decided to try to find them in the forest on foot. Ezra needed to locate Clarissa quickly—and pray that Max and his henchmen hadn't gotten to her first.

TWELVE

Clarissa wove through the trees, moving in the direction Ezra should have gone. She refused to give in to the fear that teased the corners of her mind, telling her she'd never see him again. She had to find him. From what she could tell, the forest stretched out for miles. Her plan had been to stay close to the edge where they'd both entered, but what if he had been driven deeper into the woods by the helicopter?

She stared up at the night sky. Stars twinkled back at her. The chopper noise had faded some time ago. She called Ezra's name and waited for a response. The silence fed her anxiety.

Then she heard a voice. Her renewed hope was quickly dashed when she heard a second voice answer. Max's men were on the ground, searching the forest.

Taking quick light steps, she hid behind a large tree. She pressed her back against the rough bark and held her breath. It was hard to tell how far away the men were. Their voices seemed to echo, fade and then grow louder. She shivered from fear, squeezing her eyes shut and focusing on her breathing. She heard noises that could be someone creeping past her about twenty feet away.

Clarissa pressed harder against the rough bark of the tree and looked at the sky peeking through the tree canopy.

What if it's Ezra moving past me?

After a long time of not hearing anything, she angled around the tree, but saw only shadows. An owl hooted somewhere in the distance. She stepped out, moving slowly at first and then breaking into a run. She slapped branches out of the way as she pushed harder. She ran, putting distance between herself and the direction she thought the men had been traveling.

A long time later she stopped, breathless and exhausted. "Ezra!" She yelled his name, knowing that it might bring danger to her.

"Clarissa."

Relief spread through her as he stepped out from among the trees. She ran toward him and fell into his arms.

"I found you." She couldn't hide her joy.

His arms encircled her. "Yes," he whispered. He pulled back, looked down at her and touched her cheek with his palm. "You found me."

She could feel the heat of attraction between them and it frightened her. She'd let her emotions get the best of her. Old fears returned, and she pulled away. What would another kiss between them mean? It could only open the door to heartache.

Ezra took a step back. "We've gotta get out of here." He had stripped his voice of the affection she'd heard earlier.

"I know. I heard them walking around." She pointed. "Back behind me."

He stepped closer to her, his shoulder brushing against hers. The heat of the previous moment returned. His touch had that effect on her.

"I know how we can get away. Come this way." He moved through the trees, and she followed.

He didn't reach back to hold her hand as he'd done before. She didn't blame him. She'd thrown cold water on their moment. She did like him. He was the most honorable man she'd ever met. Yet every time she thought about opening her heart to him, fear reared its ugly head. She mentally replayed memories of waiting in a bus station for twelve hours for her baby's father to show up, because he had promised to come back to her. After the last possible bus had pulled away from the curb, she'd gone into the restroom and hid in a stall, pounding the metal door as the words repeated in her mind. *Never again. Never again.*

Ezra led her to the edge of the forest through the darkness. She kept her eyes focused on the pale blur of the backpack bobbing in front of her. The terrain grew rockier and steeper, until finally Ezra stopped.

"There's a cave that winds partway through the mountain and comes out at the side. I don't think they'll look for us there."

She stumbled and almost fell. "I'm not a real fan of caves. Is there any other way?"

He released a little laugh. "After everything we've been through, it's a cave that trips you up?"

"I don't have a dramatic story connected with it. I just don't like cold, dark places." A chill ran over her at the thought of having to spend any time in a cave.

Ezra dumped the pack to the ground and pulled out the length of rope he taken from the ATV. "We'll stay tied together until we're deep enough in to turn on the light without being seen from the outside."

The description of what he had planned only made her more anxious.

"Everyone has a fear they need to face, Clarissa." He wrapped the rope around her waist and cinched it. His hand brushed over her stomach, reminding her of the power his touch held.

"What do you fear, Ezra?"

He let out a huff of air. "I fear women who are afraid of caves."

Clarissa laughed in spite of her growing uneasiness. Ezra could use humor to avoid a heartfelt answer as easily as she could.

Once the rope was secure around her waist, he tugged on it to test it. The tug brought her face closer to his. He stood near enough for her to feel his breath on her cheek. His head bent toward hers and lingered there a moment.

She couldn't read his expression in the darkness. Was he still feeling the sting of her earlier rejection? Or had it not meant anything to him?

He looped the rope through his belt and reached down for the backpack. "We'll go slow. Test the terrain in front of you before you take a step. Let me know if you're having trouble keeping up."

He led her toward what looked like shadows on the rock until she reached out and felt the cool, smooth surface of an opening in the mountain. They stepped inside, letting darkness surround them.

Just as the cave swallowed Clarissa and him up, Ezra heard two men emerge from the trees, shouting at each other. In response, he and Clarissa moved through the darkness without speaking. Voices tended to echo. They couldn't risk even whispering, not this close to the mouth of the cave. Not with those men right outside. He stepped forward, feeling the rocks beneath his feet, stepping around the larger ones.

The line between him and Clarissa went taut. He stopped, reaching for her hand in the darkness. He gave it a squeeze, and she responded in kind, but he could tell she was trembling. He wrapped his fingers around hers, hoping to offer her some reassurance.

Up to this point, she'd been fearless. She'd faced men with guns without falling apart, but the cave was the thing that finally tripped her up. He had to hand it to her. She was the most complex woman he'd ever met.

She wanted to know what he feared. Why had he deflected her question? He had traveled halfway across the world, survived in the most impossible circumstances and looked murderers in the eye. But the thing that scared him most was being hurt by a woman again.

He'd nearly given in to his desire to kiss Clarissa, to hold her. It was a good thing she'd pulled away and doused the heat of the moment. What good could acting on his attraction do anyway?

Their circumstances were precarious. That might be what was fueling the attraction, in any case. Once they were safe in town—and he would see to it that that happened—she'd probably want nothing to do with him.

He turned slightly. Light from outside no longer reached them. He stopped and pulled the flashlight out of a side pocket of the pack. He clicked it on, shining the beam toward Clarissa, but not directly in her face.

"At last, some light," she said.

"You doing okay?"

"Now I am." She turned slightly. "This is pretty level here, not too hard to walk on."

He shone the light around. "It's a tunnel that the trains used to go through. You can't see much of the tracks from years of debris falling on them."

"It shouldn't be too hard for us, then." Her voice held a note of hope.

"Actually, sorry to be the bearer of bad news, but it's caved in toward the far end. We'll take another passage that leads upward."

She didn't answer for a long time. When she did speak, her voice was barely a whisper. "Can't be helped, can it?"

"We can at least take the rope off." He reached toward her waist.

"I can get it." His fingers brushed hers as they both reached for the rope at the same time. She took a step back. "I can untie a knot."

Heat rose up his neck from the power of the moment. He needed to forget about whatever emotions she was stirring up inside him, clear his mind and focus on ensuring they both stayed alive. He'd done it a thousand times in combat. Why was this so much harder?

"Why don't we need the rope anymore?"

"It's wide and flat here, so we can walk side by side," Ezra said. "Keep talking so I'll know where you are. I'll do the same."

"You mean you're going to turn off the flashlight."

"We'll have to conserve battery power. I don't want to risk not having light when we really need it."

"More darkness." Fear returned to her voice.

"You'll thank me when we have light to get through the trickier spots." They walked for several feet side by side before he switched off the light. "Just keep talking to me, Clarissa."

"I don't know what to talk about. The weather? The stock market?" Her voice still trembled.

He laughed. "All that seems really unimportant right now, doesn't it?"

Clarissa gasped suddenly, and he heard her stumble.

He stopped and reached out for her in the darkness. "Clarissa?" He touched her shoulder.

"Just a rock that I didn't feel." Her fingers brushed over his forearm and then gripped his hand. It warmed his heart that holding his hand made her feel safer.

They walked on the level ground for maybe another twenty minutes before Ezra stopped to pull out his flashlight and assess where they were. The light revealed bats, and moisture dripping from the roof of the cave.

Clarissa edged closer to him.

"Sometimes it's better not to see what's in the dark."

She let out a nervous laugh.

"The good news is we're about ten minutes away from the surface." He dropped the pack on the ground and rifled through it, looking for something he could use to fasten the flashlight to his head so he'd have two hands free to climb.

Clarissa knelt beside him. "That means there must be some bad news."

"The bad news is it will be the hardest ten minutes of your life. It's a pretty steep climb." He pulled out a roll of medical tape before shining the light toward her. "I have every confidence you'll make it through. Help me fasten this light to my head." He handed her the tape.

She looked down at the tape and laughed. "Really? Talk about having a MacGyver moment."

"Survival is all about using what is at hand," he said.

Clarissa's eyes brightened. She might not like the darkness of the cave, but knowing she was at least temporarily safe from the thugs seemed to help her relax a little.

"I'll hold the flashlight in place. You wrap the tape around my head and under my chin."

She leaned toward him. With a touch as delicate as butterfly wings, she secured the flashlight in place. Her fingers brushed over his cheek and under his chin, causing a buzzing, dizzy sensation.

Focus, Ezra.

"Did I do okay?" Her face was only inches from his.

Why did she make him feel like he was a clumsy seventeen-year-old kid again? He wiggled the flashlight on top of his head. "I think it will stay secure."

She tilted her head toward the hole Ezra had shone a light on earlier. "How is this going to work?"

"I'll go first. We'll be tied together as a safety

measure. I know you won't be able to see real well, but try to use the same foot and handholds that I use. We have to choose them carefully. The last thing we need is a bunch of rocks coming down on us."

He tied the rope around his waist and then around hers. There was risk in this plan, too. If she fell, he might be pulled down by her momentum, but he didn't like the idea of having no way to save her if she slipped or a foothold gave way.

"Have you done this before?" She raised her arms so he could knot the rope around her waist.

"Yeah, but with better equipment and expert climbers. And we were descending from the outside, not ascending from the inside."

"I suppose it's good to change things up a bit, huh?"

He appreciated her optimism and attempt at lightening the moment. She must have picked up on the hesitation he felt over the plan. It was always experienced climbers and spelunkers he took through this. Yet what choice did he have now? This was the fastest route out and the best way to avoid detection.

It had been hours since they'd had anything to drink or eat. They needed to get out of here as quickly as possible and at least find water.

He checked the rope. "It's loose. I don't want it to cut through your skin if you get hung up."

They set off slowly. The tunnel narrowed to about three feet in diameter, forcing them to go up the gradual incline on their hands and knees. Loose rock transformed into slabs and a steeper, nearly vertical climb. When Ezra shone the light in Clarissa's direction, he saw the strain on her face as she pushed off from a foothold.

A needle-thin band of light filtered through the darkness, renewing his strength. "Almost there." His biceps strained as he dragged himself upward.

Clarissa screamed when her foot suddenly slipped, leaving her dangling. Her weight pressed the rope against his stomach. He gripped the rope with his free hand to lessen the pressure. "Get a foothold." She swung back toward the wall of rock. The pressure let up on the rope, making it clear that she'd followed his command. His voice echoed down the vertical tunnel. "How are you doing?"

"Tired." She sounded out of breath.

"I can see daylight. Tell you what. Are you secure where you're at?" The flashlight only partially illuminated her.

"Yes, I think so." He heard rocks crashing one over the other. "It feels pretty solid."

He untied the rope from around his waist.

"I'm going to crawl the rest of the way out and then pull you up. You'll still have to climb some. Loop the rope underneath your bottom."

He held on to the rope and pulled himself up the remaining distance. Daylight assaulted his eyes. They had run through the night. He yelled down the hole, "Almost there." He anchored the rope around a large rock.

The line went taut. He dug in his heels and pulled. Then it went slack, indicating she'd found a foothold and was climbing. He peered down the hole. Clarissa's dirt-stained face came into view. Her expression brightened when she saw him.

He pulled harder on the rope, one hand over the other, until she was within reach. Then he stretched out a hand to pull her the remaining distance. She let go of the wall of the cave with one hand, and their fingers touched. He leaned forward to get a tighter grip.

"Give me both hands. I can pull you straight up." His muscles strained to hold on to her.

She seemed reluctant to let go of the wall.

"You'll still be held by the rope," he assured her.

She pushed away from the wall. His first attempt to grab her other hand failed. Her eyes went wide with fear. He leaned farther into the hole of the cave, grabbing her hand and then leaning back. He heaved her up and into his arms.

She wrapped her arms around his neck, shuddering and shaking.

He held her close. "I've got you. It's okay."

She squeezed his neck tighter. "I thought I was going to fall."

He rubbed her upper back. "I wouldn't let that happen, Clarissa." He held her until she stopped shaking.

She pulled back, blue eyes resting on him. In the early-morning light, even with the smudges of dirt on her face, she was beautiful.

"I said I'd get you out of there and I did. You can trust me." The power of her gaze held him in a force field. He couldn't look away if he'd wanted to. His throat constricted as he took in a breath and cupped his hands under her jaw. His lips brushed lightly over hers. She responded to his kiss, angling her head and leaning closer to him.

Her touch electrified his skin all the way down to his toes. He kissed her more intensely, covering her mouth with his. He dropped his arm to her back and pulled her close. He held her for a long moment, arms wrapped completely around her. His lips brushed over her silky soft hair. The warmth of the early-morning sun surrounded them.

He'd avoided kissing her before, afraid of what it might mean. Even now as he held her, he was concerned that she didn't truly have feelings for him—that her desire had been fueled by the intensity of the situation they faced. She'd been up against the possibility of falling, even dying, in the cave. When he got her to a safe place, would she still have such a fiery and intense attraction to him? Did she want him because she needed his protection, or because she cared about him?

He held her, relishing the moment, the warmth of her body against his, and tried not to think about what it all would mean when they were back in Discovery.

The reverie dissipated when harsh male voices drifted up to the ledge where they rested. Ezra pulled free of their embrace and gazed below.

THIRTEEN

When Ezra pulled away to peer over the edge of the ledge, Clarissa tried to restore strength to muscles that the power of his kiss had turned to wax. She felt as though warm honey covered her skin from head to toe. She was still floating in the euphoria of his kiss when the sharp voices of the men below jerked her back into reality.

Max's men were oblivious to who was sixty feet above them. Both of them had rifles. They wore hats. She couldn't see their faces, but neither one sounded like Don or Zeke. She shifted closer to hear them more clearly, and a sprinkle of dirt rolled down the ledge toward the trail.

Ezra pulled her back toward the rock wall behind them. His hand around her waist and his chest pressing against her shoulder reignited the emotion his kiss had created.

"Thought I heard something." Down below, the men had stopped walking. "What do you suppose is up there?"

"Probably some wild animal," said the second man.

"That ledge is steep. How would they get that high up?"

Clarissa willed herself to become a statue. The slightest movement might make the men suspicious. The steady inhale and exhale of Ezra's breathing surrounded her. His proximity was a reminder of the moment they'd shared. As the thugs continued to debate down below, she lifted her gaze toward him. He offered her a slight upturn of his mouth. His brown eyes held warmth.

Believing that trusting in love only led to pain, she'd buried any desire for romance somewhere deep. But Ezra had managed to break through, to unearth what she had vowed she would never feel again. She had never wanted to be as vulnerable as she'd been at fifteen. Yet even as fear marred the memory of their kiss and being held, of feeling safe in his arms, the tiniest sprig of hope blossomed inside her. Was it possible that there were men who kept their word? The notion was far outside any frame of reference she'd ever had.

When the two men below decided to continue down the trail, Ezra did not avert his gaze from her. She stared into the ocean of mystery his eyes held, and wondered if a man like him could love her.

The voices of the thugs finally faded. Ezra let out a breath and moved away from her. "I think they're gone."

"Will we have to go down that trail?"

He rose to his feet and studied the landscape below. "There's another way we can go. Around the side of the mountain and down the other side."

She came and stood beside him. "Won't that take longer?"

"Yes, but it'll be safer. Now that we know which way they're headed, we can avoid them altogether." The two of them stood shoulder to shoulder. The back of his hand touched hers, and for a moment, she thought he would hold her hand. Not to lead her out of some danger, but as a sign of affection. Instead, he shifted his weight so their shoulders were no longer touching. She wondered what the kiss had meant to him. Had it been impulsive, like their first kiss, spurred on by the trauma of getting out of the cave alive? Or did it mean something more to him?

She cleared her throat. "Okay, so we go the long way. I'll trust your judgment on that."

"Let's get moving. The first thing we've got to do is find some water."

Out here in the wilderness, she trusted her life to him. He had shown a level of competence, savvy and strength that proved he was dependable. Trusting him with her heart, though, was entirely another matter.

Ezra led Clarissa down a narrow trail. Down below, they could see the tops of trees, and beyond that, a river. It would take them most of the day to get down the mountain and another half day to get to New Irish. They needed to find water before that—and he wasn't certain where to look. While it was true that taking this path would bring them out on the opposite side of the mountain from where they had seen Max's men, Ezra was uncertain about finding water sources.

He knew this part of the country from maps he'd studied, not from experience. He had withheld that information from Clarissa. She had enough to worry about.

She stopped suddenly. "What's that noise?" Fear flashed in her eyes.

He quit walking, trying to figure out what she had heard. "Was it…the helicopter?" Of course Max would come back looking for them with that thing. There would be no way to avoid it.

Clarissa turned slightly, facing up the mountain. "No, it was more a banging noise."

He listened, at first hearing only the wind. And then he heard the familiar sound. He shook his head and smiled. "Mountain goats."

"Mountain goats?" Her voice was tinged with fear.

"That's a good thing. If there are mountain goats around here, there has to be a water source close by." The noise had come from the west. "We'll have to go off the trail and up."

She nodded and followed him toward the sound. The high mountain terrain grew rockier, with less vegetation. The clatter of the mountain goats butting heads floated on the wind from time to time, allowing Ezra to adjust their direction.

They climbed over a ledge, and the goats came into view. Two rams wandered on one of the larger rock surfaces. Ewes and their lambs were scattered among the rocky ledges. Many of them blended with the light-colored stone, not visible until they moved.

Clarissa said, "Wow."

"They are neat animals," Ezra whispered. "We'll go around them. The less we disturb them, the better."

She continued to shake her head. "They're amazing."

He held out his hand, uncertain if she would take it. He saw a momentary hesitation, but then she laid her soft fingers in his callused hand. Her touch sent a fiery charge through him and reminded him of the kiss they'd shared.

He dismissed the heat rising up his neck. This was purely practicality. She needed help getting up the steeper part of the mountain. At least that's what he told himself.

They scaled the smooth slabs of rock while Ezra searched for a water source. "There's got to be a mountain spring around here somewhere."

"You don't know if there is for sure?" she said.

"Our expeditions never went this high up the mountain," he said.

He hoped they hadn't wasted valuable time by getting off the trail.

She released a little laugh. "You know so much about this area, I assumed you knew everything."

"I'm not all-knowing."

"You kind of had me fooled." Her voice was filled with admiration.

He shook his head as his cheeks warmed. He stood up as they came to a wide, nearly level ledge. "I don't know everything about these mountains, but God knows."

"God?" Understanding came into her eyes. "He's involved in this, too, isn't He?"

"If you don't mind, I'd like to pray to God to show us where that spring is."

She nodded again. "Okay."

He closed his eyes. "God, we're very thirsty. If it be Your will, if You could lead us to a water source, that would be great." He paused before saying amen.

When he looked up, Clarissa's expression had a soft quality and admiration shone in her eyes. "You're pretty tight with Him."

Ezra nodded. "How about you?"

"Just getting to know Him. Still learning."

"Tough first lesson, huh?" She continued to nod and gaze at him, the glow in her features never diminishing. "Let's go see how God answered that prayer," he said.

They worked their way farther up the mountain with still no sign of water. His stomach had begun to growl. This high up, there wasn't even much vegetation. Sometimes God answered a prayer and the answer was no. Without water, they'd make it off the mountain and to the river, but their strength would be sapped, and they would be in no condition for any sort of confrontation with Max or his hired muscle. Plus they'd have wasted valuable time heading the wrong direction.

Clarissa grabbed his arm and pointed to a rock slab down below. "There."

He scanned the area, not sure what she was so excited about.

"The reflection from the sun. There's water in that indentation in the rock. It must be from the storm a few days ago."

Grateful for Clarissa's sharp eyes, Ezra headed toward where she had pointed, lifting her down one of the steep rock formations before they came to the tiny pool of water. "God provides," he said. "We just can't dictate to Him how He provides."

"Water is water," she said.

He pulled her ragged pack off his back and found the water filter right away. Though the canteen had been damaged, they still had the metal cup. "The filter works like a straw. You can have the first drink."

She filled the cup, put the filter in it and drank until it was empty. "That's so wonderful." She handed him the cup and wiped her mouth. "My throat was really dry."

The water tasted sweeter than honey as it traveled down his parched throat. They drank several more cups. Clarissa touched her cheek. "Do I have dirt smudges on my face?"

He nodded his head and half smiled.

Her mouth turned up, as well. "I know it's kind of silly, but I would like to at least have a clean face."

He tore off the cloth cover from the damaged canteen, dipped it in the water and handed it to her. She washed her face and then looked at him. "Better?"

He nodded.

"You have some smears, too." She reached over and brushed the cloth over his forehead and cheeks. Her touch turned his insides to mush. He studied every angle of her face, the clear pale skin and her soft, blue-eyed gaze.

Ezra lifted the damaged canteen and turned it over in his hands. The bullet had gone clean through, creating two holes near the bottom.

"Maybe there's something else in there we can use to carry water in." The look of hopeful desperation on Clarissa's face was endearing.

He shook his head, knowing that there probably wasn't. He searched the pack anyway, for her sake. After a fruitless hunt, he refastened the pack. "Have one more drink if you want. We'll have to make it down the mountain without water."

As they worked their way off the rocky mountaintop, two things plagued his thoughts. He worried that Max would be able to locate them with his helicopter. Also, he wondered why they hadn't seen a single search plane. If the others had been rescued, a search party would have been sent to find him and Clarissa. He hadn't even spotted a rescue plane in the distance, looking for them in the wrong place.

He kept his dark thoughts to himself. He didn't know anything for sure, and if Clarissa thought the others hadn't made it out, she would lose all hope.

By midday the trees down below looked more like trees and less like dark smears. They must be at least halfway down the mountain. Fatigue lay like a heavy coat on Clarissa's body, and she found herself starting to nod off even as she continued to put one foot in front of the other.

Ezra touched her shoulder from behind. "Hey, how about we veer off the trail and get a couple hours of sleep? It would be better for us to rest now and travel under cover of night."

As anxious as she was to get into the concealment the trees provided, she didn't have the strength to argue with him. He led her to a level spot where some brush grew.

"You rest." He tore the pack off. "Use this for a pillow."

"Aren't you going to sleep, too?"

"I'm going to see if I can find us something to eat."

For the past hour, the gnawing hunger in her belly had made it hard to think of anything but food. Still, it didn't seem right that he should be deprived of the chance to rest. "Maybe I should go with you."

"No, sleep. I'll catch some shut-eye after I've found us some lunch." He didn't wait around for her to answer. Instead, he disappeared deeper into the brush. Clarissa rested her head on the hard pack and closed her eyes.

Something had shifted between her and Ezra—in a good way—though neither was talking about it. She had felt such a strong connection to him when they'd prayed for water. Finding the water had been a faith builder.

She closed her eyes, trying to get comfortable on the hard ground. A soft breeze ruffled her hair. Was it possible that someone like Ezra would really care about someone like her? She didn't know if she could trust her feelings or not. She'd been down this road before.

She turned and stared at the huge blue sky above her. Maybe the second kiss had been a mistake, too. Would he get her to a safe place because that was his job? Or would he stay after all this was over?

She rolled over on her side and closed her eyes. Sleep came quickly. Her final thoughts as she drifted off were of Ezra, his soft, barely there smile and the strong arms that had held her.

She awoke with a start to the mechanical

clang of an engine. It took her a moment to absorb that a helicopter was nearby.

She rolled over on her stomach and peered through the brush. The chopper hovered at her level, angling from side to side before pointing its nose downward. It landed on a flat spot several hundred feet below her. Two men got out—Don and Zeke. After they disembarked, the chopper lifted from the ground and disappeared around the side of the mountain.

The men were headed up the trail, rifles flung over their shoulders. Clarissa craned her neck. No sign of Ezra anywhere. Staying low to the ground, she grabbed the pack and darted in the direction he'd gone. She scanned the brush and the steep hillside. No sign of him anywhere. Down below, the men were closing in, their rowdy talk growing louder and more distinct.

Clarissa slumped to the ground. It wouldn't be safe for her to wait here until Ezra showed himself. He might be hiding from the chopper, as well. She saw flashes of color through the grass from the men's clothes, yellow and red. They were getting closer.

If she made a wide arc around them and stayed off the trail, their paths would never cross, and she could get to the bottom of the mountain without being seen. She kept her radar tuned to the sound of the approaching men as she worked her way through the brush and across the open areas. The gruff voices of the two men grew dim as she headed away from them.

Fear and physical exertion made her heart pound wildly. She took in a ragged breath and then glanced over her shoulder before descending down the mountain. She only hoped that Ezra would figure out where she'd gone.

FOURTEEN

Ezra heard the helicopter before he saw the two men. From a distance, Ezra could see that Clarissa was no longer in the spot where she'd been resting. A quick scan of the area revealed that she wasn't anywhere close by. Though being separated from her caused tightness in his chest, it might be a good thing that she wasn't visible. Max's two thugs were making their way up the trail.

When he'd heard the helicopter, he'd hoped to get a glimpse of it on the off chance that it was a rescue helicopter. The chopper left the area before he ever saw it, however. Then he caught sight of the men stopped by the patch of brush where Clarissa had been sleeping. He slipped behind the rock where he'd been hiding, lifting his head high enough to watch them.

Don kicked the brush around and then held up something and showed it to the other man. An item must have fallen out of her pack. Ezra cringed. Though he couldn't hear what was said, the pointing and gestures indicated that whatever Clarissa had left behind was enough to clue them in that she was in the area.

His heart lurched as he looked around for any sign of movement that might indicate where she was. He needed to be with her, to know that she was safe. One of the men pointed down with his rifle. A moment later, both the thugs headed toward the forest.

Waiting to avoid detection was excruciating. Ezra didn't like sitting still for any reason, but the sense of urgency he felt to catch up with Clarissa made him want to jump up and run down the mountain.

He peeked out from behind the rock. The voices of the two men had faded, but he could still see the yellow and red of their shirts. He darted toward a pile of brush that would provide some cover. Keeping an awareness of the men's location, he worked his way down the mountain. Not being able to take the trail meant he was probably traveling twice the distance of the thugs, but his greater experience in hiking made him able to keep up with their pace.

The men's voices carried on the wind. Ezra dived into the tall grass as they came around a bend in the trail. He was so close he could hear their boots crunching on the pebbles. He pressed his body against the hard ground.

One of the men, the older one, stopped and peered down the mountain. "Hey." He lifted his rifle and looked through the scope. "There she is."

The air froze in Ezra's lungs, and he felt an invisible weight on his back pinning him in place. The man placed his finger on the trigger. Ezra dug his hands into the dirt, ready to pounce. Clarissa was not going to be gunned down like an animal, not on his watch.

The second thug edged toward the first. "I don't see her."

Don let the rifle fall to his side. "I saw her. She's down there."

"Let's go get her then," said Zeke. "Fitzgerald doesn't want her getting out of these woods alive."

Ezra waited only a few minutes before jumping up and heading down the mountain. The thugs had picked up the pace and now jogged down the trail. Ezra moved as quickly as he could.

He didn't want to risk being spotted himself, but he needed to get to Clarissa before the armed men did.

Though anxiety coiled in her stomach, Clarissa pushed herself to go faster. She looked over her shoulder. Still no Ezra. And then she saw the flash of yellow and red through the brush. The men were moving pretty fast down the trail. They must have spotted her.

Their voices carried on the wind. Don ordered Zeke to go in a different direction. She scanned the area for possible places to hide.

The talking had stopped, and she couldn't see either of the men. What would Ezra do if he were in her position? She studied the open field in front of her and calculated a path that would take her from one covered position to another. The last fifty yards would have to be at an all-out run. Taking in a breath, she steeled herself and sprinted toward the first patch of tall grass.

The thug in the yellow shirt, Zeke, came into view. He stopped scanning the open field as he made his way toward it. He disappeared again behind a cluster of aspen trees. She shot to her feet and ran toward some brush.

When she looked through the leaves of the bush she crouched behind, she could see both men some distance from each other but moving toward her. They were too close. There was no way she could keep running without being spotted. Clarissa flattened herself behind the bush. Though its leaves had turned gold and orange, there was still enough of them to keep her hidden from view…unless the men came too close or veered around her side of the bush. She'd be an easy target if that happened.

She decided to crawl the remaining distance. Pulling herself with her arms, she covered several feet of ground, stopped, assessed where the men were and then crawled some more. The trees were a stone's throw away when the first rifle shot passed over her head. She lurched to her feet and ran the remaining distance to a cluster of trees as another shot boomed behind her.

Ezra heard the rifle shots just as he entered the forest. He sprinted toward the sound.

Please, God, don't let her have been hit.

The shouts of the thugs pressed on his ears and a moment later the one in the yellow shirt ran past him. Ezra trailed behind the man, relieved to see him by himself. Ezra could take on one of the armed men, but not both at once. He followed Zeke, slipping behind trees every time the thug sensed his presence.

If the man was still searching, Clarissa must be alive. The thug stopped. Breathing heavily, he slumped down on a log. Ezra raced toward him. His footfalls were so soft the man didn't even turn to look around until Ezra was on top of him. He grabbed the rifle and slapped the man across the face. The thug crumpled to the ground, falling on his hands. Ezra was preparing to hit him one more time when he felt a blow to the back of his head.

Spots appeared before his eyes as he swung around to defend himself from Don. Ezra got in a solid hit to the face and blow to the man's stomach before the ground seemed to swallow him up. Pine needles prickled Ezra's skin as his vision dimmed.

"No, don't kill him," said Zeke. "I saw the woman. She's around here. This guy will make good bait."

The last thing he heard before everything went black was Don yelling, "Hey, Clarissa, we got your boyfriend!"

From high up in the tree where she'd taken refuge, Clarissa watched the two men drag Ezra's body toward an open area. She gasped. Was he dead? She gripped the branch until her knuckles turned white. Zeke disappeared into the woods.

Don pulled string out of his pack. He dragged Ezra toward a tree and propped him against it. She let out a breath. He must be alive if Don was tying him up.

Her stomach clenched into knots. Ezra had ended up in this situation only because he'd wanted to help her. She had to find a way to get him free.

She watched for over an hour as Zeke gathered wood and built a fire. The two men ate from their packs. Ezra's head jerked suddenly. She winced when he hit the back of his head on the tree trunk.

The thugs acknowledged that he had awakened, but then continued to eat. Her own stomach growled as she made her way down the tree. The men were watching their rifles closely. No doubt they'd kept Ezra alive to draw her in.

Don had nearly captured her. She gotten away when his foot had caught on a root and he'd fallen. He knew how close she was, and he knew she'd come looking for Ezra.

They'd be on high alert through the night, probably taking turns keeping watch. They might even patrol the area. She moved in a wide arc around the camp, still uncertain what she could do that wouldn't get both of them killed.

They had rifles. She had a pocketknife. There were two of them and one of her. She moved in a little closer to where the men were camped. What she needed was a moment when they were both distracted. If she could get Ezra untied…

She crawled a little nearer, to where she had a clear view of Ezra. Don had his back to him but Zeke watched their captive closely.

Ezra shifted from side to side, probably trying to get more comfortable. His hands were behind his back, angled around a narrow tree. She gripped the pocketknife. If she could get near enough to give him the knife, he could cut himself free.

She edged as close as she could while still remaining hidden by the trees. The metal pocketknife was cold to the touch. She had a clear view of the tree and his back. She had one chance to get the knife in his hands.

Don and Zeke continued to complain about how tired they were from tromping through the woods, and how Max better have a big payday for them. Zeke finally left the camp to go to the bathroom. This was her chance. She scooted out from the protection of the trees, focused on Ezra's hands and tossed the knife. It clipped his fingertips and landed a few inches away.

She ducked back into the cover of the trees. With his limited reach, Ezra patted the dirt around his hands. She tensed. Was the knife too far away? He continued to search the ground. At last she saw his fingertips touch the metal. He clawed through the dirt, grasping the handle. He had the knife.

Zeke returned. The two men continued to complain about their job. Clarissa retreated deeper into the trees while Ezra cut through the rope. She found a log with another tree fallen on top of it, the perfect hiding place. She couldn't see what was going on in the camp, but she could hear.

"Do you want some water?" Don asked Ezra.

Clarissa tensed. Would he untie Ezra for that?

Ezra's answer was slow in coming. "Sure, I could use some."

She listened to the exchange, unable to see anything from her hiding place. The sky darkened. Gradually, the loud conversation of the two men subsided. She knew Ezra was waiting for the right moment—most likely when one man was asleep and the other distracted. Ezra had probably cut through the rope ages ago.

Her legs cramped from being in such a tight space but the hiding spot was too perfect to abandon. Someone could walk by her and not see her, yet she could hear everything that was going on in the camp. A quiet settled in around her, and all she heard was the crackling of the fire. Once she nodded off. She opened and shut her eyes, then shook her head to stay awake.

Footsteps pounded past not far from her. At the camp, one of the men voiced a string of expletives. With her heart racing, Clarissa crawled out of her hiding place and headed in the general direction where she'd heard the footsteps.

She'd run only twenty yards when a hand grabbed her from the side.

"Clarissa." Ezra's voice was a song to her heart.

She fell into his arms, giving him a quick hug and wishing it could be longer. "We have to go."

Keeping hold of her hand, Ezra darted through the forest. They ran through the dark, weaving in and out of the trees. The shouts of the men behind them died down, but that didn't mean they were safe. The thugs would likely opt for the element of surprise instead of broadcasting their position.

After more than an hour of being chased, Ezra led her to a high place that provided a view of the valley below.

"There," he said, pointing to two lights bobbing through the trees. "I know how we can get away from them. Follow me."

Without a flashlight, Clarissa hung close to Ezra, stepping where he stepped. They traveled for what seemed like hours before finding a place in the forest to rest. Clarissa slumped to the ground, using a tree for a backrest.

"That was really something back there—you getting me out of there." Admiration colored his voice.

She let out a laugh. "I just asked myself what would Ezra do?"

"Is that right?" He scooted closer to her.

"I'm starving." She touched the hollow drum that was her stomach. "How much longer before we get to the river?"

"I'm hungry, too, but we don't have time to find food. We took a detour to get away from those guys, so I'd say a few hours, if we hike through the night."

Clarissa's tired muscles felt suddenly heavier. A few hours seemed like a thousand years.

"I know you're tired." His hand covered hers in the dark. He must have picked up on her emotions. Was he that tuned in to how she was feeling?

They marched on through the night. The trees thinned and opened up. Off in the distance, she saw the warm glow of lights. She blinked, wondering if she was seeing things.

"Is that what I think it is?"

FIFTEEN

Ezra stood close to Clarissa, looking out at a cabin with smoke coming out of the chimney.

"Did you know someone lived out here?"

A sense of both joy and relief spread through him. "No, I didn't. Like I said, we're a little farther west than I usually go. The cabin might only be occupied seasonally, too."

"Maybe whoever is in the cabin will have a phone we can use." Her voice was filled with hope.

He, too, was ready for this ordeal to be over. Once they got to town and spoke to the police, these men could be rounded up. Maybe then he'd be able to help Clarissa get to the bottom of why Max was so bent on killing her.

They hiked toward the cabin, losing sight of it as they descended a hill and climbed up the other side. Though he relaxed a little with a goal in sight, Ezra hadn't dropped his guard completely. The men had been persistent in chasing them, and they might have figured out where he and Clarissa had taken their detour.

"We can't stay long. I don't want to put who-ever lives here at risk."

"I know," she said. "Just time enough to use their phone, and perhaps see if they have some food we can buy."

"Yeah, I'm pretty hungry, too." He snuck a glance at her as they walked side by side, her blond hair waving in the breeze and that look of determination on her face.

His fondness for Clarissa had only grown since she'd helped him escape the two thugs. She could have kept going and gotten away. Not only had she been brave and clever, she had risked her own life to save his. Maybe she would have done it for anyone, but he liked to think it revealed a bond between them.

They approached the cabin slowly in the dark. He couldn't see a car or truck anywhere. With a cabin this remote, the owner might have to park some distance away and hike in. Through the window, he could see the glow of a burn-ing fire. No other lights were on—not that he could see anyway. They'd probably be waking the occupant or occupants.

He knocked on the door. No answer.

Clarissa grasped his arm. "I hear something. It's coming from the other side of the house."

They walked around as the sound of an ax slicing through wood became more obvious. The man splitting logs had his back to them when they came around the corner. There was no way to alert him to their presence and not scare him.

Ezra cleared his throat.

The man spun around with the ax still in his hand.

"We didn't mean to frighten you." Clarissa spoke softly.

"We saw the lights of your cabin, and we're in a bit of trouble," Ezra added. "Do you have a phone we could use?"

The man studied them for a long moment with his mouth open. "I don't have a phone. We come out here to disconnect from all that." He gathered some split wood into his arms. "Have to keep the fire going all night to keep the cabin warm. That autumn chill is something else."

Ezra picked up several of the split logs. "We can give you a hand with that."

"I suppose that would be all right." The man's shifting gaze indicated he still didn't totally trust them.

Clarissa gathered up several logs, as well. They followed the man around to the front of the house.

"You can just leave the wood on the porch." He stood leaning against the door, sizing them up.

"We're not intending to hurt you in any way," said Clarissa. "It's just that we really need some help." Her voice faltered.

The door swung open, and an older woman in a bathrobe emerged. "Henry, what's going on? I heard voices."

"These folks have gotten themselves lost, Mae," said Henry, not taking his eyes off Clarissa and Ezra. "They wanted to use our phone, but I told them we don't have one out here."

Mae looked at Clarissa, compassion welling up in her eyes. "The two of you look like you've been through the wringer. We can at least get you warmed up and give you something to eat."

"I suppose it would be all right if you came inside and got warmed up." Henry pushed the door open.

The cabin consisted of one room. An unlit kerosene lantern rested on the table beside a stack of books. A worn, comfortable-looking chair faced the fireplace. There were several coolers stacked in a corner along with some dry goods. The crackling of the fire and the heat it threw out was enticing.

"Have a seat." Mae scurried around, placing

a kettle on the wood stove. "I'll get you folks some tea."

Clarissa stepped forward. "We don't want to take up too much of your time. There are some men after us, bad men. We don't want to lead them to your door."

"Oh, you poor dears," said Mae.

Henry ran his hands through his silver-gray hair. He studied them for a long moment. Certainly, if their physical condition didn't hint at the validity of their story, the emotion in Clarissa's voice had.

Finally, the old man spoke. "Well, there is the boat."

"You have a boat? Would you still have a way of getting out of here if we used it?"

"We hiked in. Truck is about five miles up the trail." The man walked over to where his canned goods were stacked. He grabbed two cans off the shelf. "Go about two miles downriver. You'll come to a sandbar. Make sure the boat is secured. I'll find a way to get it." He handed the cans to Clarissa. "That will put you close to the farms outside of New Irish."

Clarissa wrapped her arms around Henry and hugged him. "Thank you." The man seemed embarrassed by such a show of gratitude. Color rose up in his cheeks.

Still under the cover of darkness, Ezra and

Clarissa left the cabin and found the boat at the end of a dilapidated wooden pier. Ezra untied the rope and pushed off with an oar. For a long time, the only sound was the slicing of his oar through the water as he navigated toward the other side of the river. The rippling water had a calming effect on him. The boat swayed gently back and forth. He knew he couldn't allow himself to be lulled into thinking they were safe. There were two sets of men, a helicopter and Max all roaming the mountains looking for them.

He steered the boat closer to the opposite shore. Looking over at Clarissa, he noticed that she was swiping at her eyes.

"Are you…crying?"

"I'm just tired…and a little happy, too. We're going to make it, aren't we?"

"Looks that way." They still had a long, arduous night ahead of them, but he did not want to destroy the hope that she had expressed. It was more valuable than anything they had in that backpack or any skill he possessed. Hope gave a person the strength to keep going against all odds.

"How long does it take to go two miles in a boat?"

"Hard to measure. I'm watching for that sandbar. But maybe what we should be looking for is the lights from those farmhouses," he said.

She turned so she faced the shoreline, drawing her knees up to her chest. "Peaceful out here, isn't it?"

"That's why I love my job. You really haven't gotten a chance to experience how special being out here can be."

"I'm experiencing it now." Waves lapped against the boat, creating an accompaniment to his oar cutting through the water. Clarissa's blond hair shone in the moonlight as she tilted her head toward the night sky.

Their peace was short-lived. In the distance, he saw the flashing light of the helicopter. The whirring noise of the blades grew louder as it headed straight up the river toward them.

The drone of the chopper shattered Clarissa's contentment and sent a surge of panic through her.

"Get down." Ezra paddled hard and fast, veering toward the shore. The sound of the helicopter engine drowned out all other noise.

Even before they reached the beach, Ezra jumped out of the boat and pushed it toward the shore. Clarissa got out, as well, nearly falling in the waist-deep water, but recovering enough to help pull the boat to shore.

The chopper hovered over the water. Clearly, they'd been spotted. Ezra took off running, and she followed. They raced toward a field with tall plants in it ready for harvest. In the distance, a smattering of lights dotted the landscape.

Ezra dived down between the furrows. The helicopter landed and two men got out. The chopper then circled the fields, the two thugs running in a zigzag pattern and doubling back.

Clarissa let out a slow breath. At least their pursuers hadn't seen where they were hiding. She glanced at the night sky. The helicopter wouldn't be able to spot them, either, unless they were forced out into the open.

Ezra's arm rested over her back. "Let's follow this row of alfalfa as far as it will take us."

She nodded in agreement, and together, they worked their way to the edge of the field. Beyond that was a fence, and in the distance, maybe half a mile away, a structure glowed with light and life.

"Now what?" Clarissa whispered into his ear.

"We wait," he said. "Going out into the open would be suicide."

The helicopter made several more passes. The droning and clanging of the engine sliced across Clarissa's nerves. She drew her hands into fists and rested them against her forehead.

How long could they keep doing this? She was tired, worn-out and ready to give up.

Ezra brushed his fingers over her hair, tucked a strand behind her ear and kissed her temple. "We're going to make it," he whispered.

He always seemed to know what she was feeling and how to pull her from the dark places her mind wanted to go. Gradually, the noise of the helicopter faded as the pilot searched farther away.

Now all they had to do was avoid being caught by the two men on the ground. One of them stomped by the edge of the field dangerously near to where they were lying. Clarissa tensed as her heart pounded against her rib cage. They waited. Her face pressed against the ground, and she breathed in dirt. One of the men shouted a command. The reply of the second man was dangerously close as he made his way up the row where they were hiding.

Clarissa scrambled to a different row, while Ezra rolled in the opposite direction. The thug swished the top of the alfalfa with his rifle as he drew near. Clarissa pressed her cheek against the hard earth once more. The ground vibrated with the sound of the footsteps growing closer. His polished boots were only inches from her face, which was shielded only by the tall plants and the darkness. Her throat went dry, and she feared her raging heartbeat would give her away. The moments ticked by as the boots turned slightly toward her. She clenched her teeth, not daring to take a breath or move even an eyelash.

The man stood still for what felt like a million years before stepping out and heading up toward where Ezra was hiding. The thug continued to peek between the rows of plants by pushing them aside with his rifle. She had no way to warn Ezra, and prayed that he'd moved farther back in the row.

The thug's footsteps faded. After another ten or so minutes had passed, she couldn't hear voices or footsteps. She lifted her head, not catching any sign that the men were close by. She rose to her knees and peered through the plants in all directions. Confident that they had moved on, she whispered, "Ezra."

The plants made a rustling sound and then he was beside her. "They went off that way."

"Toward the farmhouses." She couldn't hide her disappointment.

"Yeah, my guess is they will be knocking on every door, acting like policemen and saying we're fugitives. They might even be searching the places. No farmer will help us."

She glanced through the barbed wire fence. Three sets of lights glowed in the distance.

"Even if we could get to one of those farm-houses before they did, we'd endanger the lives of the people there."

"I think we'd be better off heading toward the road and trying to catch a ride into town," he said.

A wave of sadness and fatigue hit her. "How far are we from New Irish?"

"Twenty minutes if we don't catch a ride. It's another hour to get back to Discovery by car."

"If we can catch a ride before they catch us." She hung her head, fighting hard not to give in to the encroaching despair.

He covered her hand with his. "I know that seems implausible right now, but don't give up." He pressed his palm against her cheek and drew her close. "We're almost home. Three hours ago, we couldn't even see the lights of civilization. Look how far we've come."

"I'm so tired. This is hard," she said.

"I know. I am, too." His fingers brushed over her cheek. "But we need to keep moving. We've got to take advantage of the darkness while we have it." He gathered her into his arms and held her close, his strength and warmth replenishing her spent energy and renewing her hope.

He rose to his feet and held out a hand for her, pulling her up. She'd never known someone like Ezra, strong and yet capable of such a gentle response to her discouragement. She supposed that was what made him a good leader—his ability to talk people off their emotional ledges. And he probably would have made the maximum effort to save her life no matter who she was. But she'd like to believe that there was something more driving his responses to her than a sense of duty. She certainly felt the stirrings of affection in her heart. For the first time in ten years, she entertained the possibility that love could come into her life.

They walked on until they entered a field where the hay had been harvested and rolled into huge cylindrical bales. Ezra stopped. "Let's take a break and eat the canned goods Henry gave us."

Clarissa slumped down to the ground beside a bale. Ezra handed her a can with a pull-off top. He rooted through the pack. "Do you suppose your spoon survived all this backpack has been through?"

She leaned close to him. "I don't know." The bag had new holes and tears from all the rough treatment. She took it and felt around. The water filter was still there as well as a cup. Her fingers grazed over the money she had stuffed in an inner pocket.

Just over a week ago, she'd been wearing nice suits, eating at expensive restaurants and sailing down the freeways of Los Angeles. Now she was searching a dirty, torn backpack, hoping to find a utensil so she didn't have to eat with her fingers.

She recovered a spoon and a fork. "I have peaches. What do you have to eat?"

Ezra squinted in the dim light. "Looks like pork and beans."

"We'll share." She stabbed a peach with her fork and moved it toward his mouth.

"Mmm…sweet." He offered her a spoonful of beans.

After they finished eating, she rested her head against his shoulder. "Can we just stay here a moment longer?"

Ezra tilted his face toward the sky, probably calculating how long they had until dawn. "It wouldn't hurt to catch our breath."

"What are you thinking about?" he asked.

"About my life in L.A. How it's all gone… everything but my faith."

"You miss it."

"No, I guess not," she said. "If we get to town, and we're able to prove that Max is behind all this, he'll go to jail, which is where he clearly belongs. I wouldn't want to undo it all and go back to working for him. I just don't know what happens next in my life."

"What do you mean?"

"My whole life since I was fifteen, all my energy and focus, went into working, to get ahead and not ever be hungry again."

He leaned back against the hay bale. "So you go back to work. Sounds like you have lots of skills and experience."

She stared up at the stars. "I'm starting to think there must be something more for me than focusing on work." For the first time in ten years, she was beginning to wonder if she could dare hope for a husband and a family. "Do you ever think about that?"

"I used to. With the kind of job I have, what kind of woman would put up with me?" The tone of his voice changed, hinting at some deep anger. "Work is enough for me."

Clarissa crumbled inside. Ezra couldn't have been more clear. She'd taken a risk, put her heart out there, and his response had proved that he wasn't interested. She wouldn't do that again. She purged her voice of all emotion. "I suppose we should get going."

They walked for several hours. Clarissa nursed the deep hurt that was like a knife through her. As the sun rose up over the mountains, the country road came into view.

SIXTEEN

To Ezra the road was a welcome sight. Traffic would be light this time of day, but hopefully, someone would go by who'd be willing to give them a lift. Max's men had assumed they'd headed toward the farmhouses, which bought them some time. But sooner or later the thugs would figure out where they had gone.

Clarissa had been quiet since they left the hayfield, and Ezra hadn't really felt like talking, either. Her question about marriage and family had brought up the old pain connected with Emma. Thinking about her only made him angry.

"I hear a truck." Clarissa grabbed his arm and pointed at the dust cloud up the road.

"Let's hope he stops." If the driver didn't pick them up, they might be walking on this road for a while, which left them dangerously exposed. They couldn't stay out in the open like this for long.

Clarissa had shown admirable strength through this whole trauma, but he could tell that her emotions were wearing thin. He needed to get her back to Discovery.

The truck loaded with rectangular hay bales came into view. It whizzed past them, but stopped about twenty yards up the road. Ezra ran ahead. A black-and-white border collie stuck his head out the passenger side window and barked.

"You hush up now, Bart." The man was clean-cut, with streaks of gray in his black, curly hair. The dog sat back on its haunches at the command but continued to eye Ezra with suspicion.

"We could use a ride." Not wanting to rile the dog up again, Ezra stood back from the window.

"Where to?"

"New Irish," Ezra said.

"I'm taking a load of hay into Discovery."

"Sir, that would be even better." The end to their flight was getting closer by the minute.

The man seemed to be sizing Ezra up when he noticed the military patch on his jacket. "Marine Corps, huh?"

"Two tours in Iraq, sir."

"I go back a little further than that." Any suspicion the man had seemed to melt. "Why don't you and your friend get up in the cab? If Bart can stand you, I can stand you."

"Deal." Ezra waved Clarissa over. "He'll take us."

"What's your name, son?"

"Ezra Jefferson."

The man tipped his baseball hat. "Steven Gould."

Clarissa stood beside Ezra as he opened the door. Bart offered her a warm reception, licking her face and sitting on her lap when she crawled into the cab.

"Bart tends to like women," said Steven. "Men he's not so sure about."

Ezra scooted in beside her. As the truck rumbled down the road, he searched the sky for signs of the helicopter, but saw nothing.

Steven drove through the tiny town of New Irish and turned onto the highway. The conversation was mostly about both men's military experience. Even though Ezra and Clarissa probably looked awful, Steven didn't ask any questions about what had brought them to that stretch of road in the early-morning hours. The dotted yellow lines clipped by. The tension that had coiled around Ezra's chest for days loosened up.

The skyline of Discovery, the tall buildings of the university, came into view. "Where do you folks want to be dropped off?"

"The police station?" Ezra looked to Clarissa for confirmation.

Her eye twitched nervously, but she nodded. "Yes, I guess that would be best."

Steven pulled the truck over to the curb across from the station and wished them well before driving off.

As she stared at the police station, Clarissa's expression clouded and a furrow formed between her eyebrows.

"Like I said before, this is a good bunch of police officers. Max couldn't have polluted everyone's mind with his lies and false accusations."

"I hope you're right." She looked at Ezra, her voice taking on an anxious tone. "We need to find out if the others made it down the mountain."

His thoughts had run in the same direction as they'd drawn closer to town. He would never forgive himself for choosing to split up if the other four didn't make it out. "We'll deal with the Max situation first, and then I'll call my partner and find out if the others showed up."

They walked to the curb and waited to cross the street. Clarissa let out a gasp and took two steps back. Fear colored her every word. "It's him. That's Don's car." She pointed to a rental car parked in front of the police station.

"Are you sure?" Ezra stared at the car, and

at a man with his back to them standing on the lawn outside the police station. The man did look like the one who had chased them over the past few days. "They must have figured we'd show up here after they lost us outside of New Irish."

"We can't go into that police station," she said.

He grabbed her wrist. "He's not going to try anything in broad daylight." Ezra glanced around. It was still two hours before the shops opened up. The streets were deserted.

"Please, I can't go in there." He'd never seen her this frantic. "You don't know what that man tried to do to me." She shook her head. "I can't believe we've come this far…only to have this happen. He's turning around." She darted up the street and Ezra followed, careful not to look over his shoulder and give them away.

Clarissa slowed her pace to a fast walk to keep from calling attention to herself. Ezra pulled her into the first alley they came to.

"Do you think he saw us?" She still hadn't calmed down.

"I don't know, and I don't want to wait around to find out. We've got to hide somewhere they won't be expecting us to go."

"Do you have a friend we could go to?"

"No one who lives within walking distance."

He tugged on her sleeve. "Let's keep moving. We'll stay off the main streets."

They hurried down another alley. "I don't even see a coffee shop open."

"Just keep walking." The back entrances of the commercial buildings were all dark. They walked past a men's clothing shop, a diner and an art gallery.

A man came out on the fire escape above them, and Clarissa jumped. Ezra put his hand on her shoulder. "It's all right," he soothed.

They stopped for a moment when they heard voices on the main street. Ezra peered around the building. Don stood talking on his phone. Ezra heard only bits and pieces of the conversation, but gathered that Don had seen them and was calling for help in the search. Ezra gazed around, trying to think of what would be open at this hour or where they could hide. If Max's goons were watching the police station, they were probably also watching his office.

"It's only a matter of time before the other three start swarming in," she said.

"I say we keep moving," Ezra said.

She slipped her hand in his. "Okay, you probably know this town better than I do."

"Oh, yeah, how long did you live here?" He thought if he could keep her talking she'd calm down.

"A little over a year, I guess. I came here with my foster family."

"That didn't work out?"

"They were nice enough people, but…it's a long story."

"We've got time for stories."

"It's not a story I want to tell." Her tone had become defensive. They hurried past another art gallery.

"There." He pointed across the street to a twenty-four hour self-serve laundry. They waited at the light and then crossed. The glass storefront wouldn't exactly hide them, but at least they wouldn't be out in the open. As they stepped inside, Ezra glanced up the street. He thought he saw one of the thugs about two blocks away.

Inside, the air was humid. Two dryers tossed clothes around. A single washing machine chugged away. Whoever had loaded the clothes must have stepped out for a cup of coffee or something.

Ezra walked over to a bin of clothes that had been left behind. He stared down at his muddy shirt. "We kind of stand out dressed like this." He grabbed a baseball hat and a blouse from the bin and tossed them to her. Then he rooted around until he found a men's button-down shirt and cotton jacket that looked as if they might fit him.

Both of them changed in their respective bathrooms. Clarissa pulled the hat down over her face.

She sized up Ezra when he came out into the main area. He tugged at the collar of his shirt, obviously not used to having to wear such stiff fabric. "It's kind of itchy, but what do you think?" he asked earnestly.

A slight smile graced her face. "I think you feel a little more at home in a worn flannel shirt and jeans."

They stepped out the front door. The streets were still mostly deserted. "We need to get somewhere where we can make some calls. I've gone fishing with one of the police officers. If I can talk to him directly maybe he can bring us in safely."

Clarissa scanned the streets. She took in a breath as though working up the courage to speak. "I think I know where we can go to be safe and make some calls. There's a place about six blocks from here. It's called Naomi's Place. I know the woman who runs it. If it's still open, she'll let us in and help us."

"I've heard of it. It hasn't closed down," he said. It was a shelter for pregnant teens. He could only guess at why Clarissa knew about it.

He surveyed the street again. His eyes grew suddenly wide. He grabbed Clarissa and pulled her around to the side of the building.

"Did you see one of them?" The stress in her voice revved up a notch.

"Yeah, I'm pretty sure I did. The four of them and maybe even Max are crawling all over the neighborhood looking for us. I have a plan. Our clothes are different. They're not going to recognize us from a distance. Two of us together, though, will be a red flag."

"So you're saying we split up and meet at Naomi's Place." Her heart beat a little faster.

He nodded. "Are you up to doing that?"

Fear encroached on every fiber of her being, but she managed to nod. "It shouldn't take us more than ten minutes to walk there."

He kissed her forehead and squeezed her hand. "I'll see you in ten minutes then."

They walked around to the front of the laundry and took off in different directions. Clarissa peered out from beneath the brim of her hat, surveying the area around her. Zeke stalked up the street across from her, moving in the opposite direction, his red hair easy to spot. She kept her pace even while her heart pounded wildly and sweat snaked down her neck. She pretended to be interested in something she saw in a shop window before moving on toward the light.

Zeke continued to work his way up the street, peering down alleys and in open shops. When the light turned, she crossed the street. The red-headed thug was two blocks up on the same sidewalk as her. She hurried down a side street. When she was finally out of view, she stopped, pressed her back against a wall and took in a frantic breath.

She walked briskly the rest of the way, turning down a residential street and breathing a sigh of relief when the converted schoolhouse that was now Naomi's Place came into view. A whirlwind of memories rushed toward her, some of them good and some painful. Coming here would open the door for Ezra to know about her past. She had chosen Naomi's Place for a reason. Not only would they be safe there, but it would give her a chance to tell Ezra about all that she had been through. After all he'd done for her, he deserved to know the truth about her past.

She opened the chain-link gate. There was no sign of Ezra on either side of the street. Her rib cage tightened with fear. She only hoped he had made it without getting caught.

SEVENTEEN

Ezra was glad to see Clarissa waiting outside Naomi's Place as he came around the corner.

She made her way up the steps, and he joined her.

"So this is Naomi's Place. I've seen the ads around town," he said.

She raised her hand to knock but stopped and looked at him, allowing her arm to drop to her side. "I stayed here when I was a teenager. My foster family kicked me out when they learned I was pregnant, and Naomi took me in. I miscarried. That was probably the saddest day of my life."

Compassion welled up in him as he reached out for her hand. "You've been through so much." He couldn't read the expression on her face. The brightness of her eyes seemed to dim, and he sensed that she was retreating emotionally.

She turned her head away. "I don't want your pity." She knocked on the door.

He let out a heavy breath. "It's not pity. It's admiration for the person you've become despite that."

Before she could respond, the door swung open. An older woman with salt-and-pepper hair, a long narrow nose and a soft smile stood on the threshold.

"Naomi," said Clarissa.

The older woman looked at her for a long moment as recognition spread across her face. "Clarissa." She gathered her into her arms. "My little lost lamb. I didn't know if I would ever see you again."

Naomi held her for a long moment, stroking her hair. Finally, Clarissa pulled free of the hug and wiped her eyes.

Naomi looked at Ezra. "And who is this?"

Clarissa seemed to be at a loss for words as she glanced at Ezra and then back at Naomi. A tear rolled down her cheek.

"I'm Ezra Jefferson. I'm her...her friend." He stepped forward. "We don't want to disrupt your day. We only need to borrow your phone."

"Sure, why don't you come in? The girls are just finishing up breakfast. I can bring you some food if you'd like."

"That would be great. We're famished." Ezra placed a supportive hand on Clarissa's back as they stepped inside a large, narrow room with an assortment of couches and chairs that had seen a little wear.

Naomi pointed to a door off to the side. "You can use my office to make your phone call."

She disappeared through another door. The sound of female laughter rose up from a distant room, but was cut off when Naomi shut the door.

Though she had stopped crying, Clarissa still seemed emotionally wrecked. Ezra opened the door to the office and allowed her to go in first. The room had a desk that was barely visible beneath all the stacks of books, papers in file folders and photo albums. Clarissa slumped down on a couch pushed against the wall opposite the desk.

He grabbed a box of Kleenex off the desk and sat down beside her. "So this place is stirring up a lot of memories for you, isn't it?"

She nodded, wiping her nose with a tissue. "Mostly good ones. They were kind to me here. I made two really good friends." She covered her eyes with her hands. "Shouldn't we make that phone call?"

Seeing her cry caused his own emotions to unravel. "We will do that. I want to make sure you're okay first."

"It's not something that is going to be okay

in ten minutes, Ezra." She rose to her feet and stared out the window by the desk.

"Tell me what you're thinking."

"When I saw Naomi, it brought back the memories of the baby and all the dreams I had. You know, to be married and have a family," she said.

"You can still have that."

He caught the flash of hurt that crossed her features. She shook her head. "You don't understand."

He got up from the couch and stood beside her. "What don't I understand?"

"Let's make the phone call, okay?" Her words had a sharp edge to them.

"What don't I understand, Clarissa?"

"Being with you…has changed something for me." She turned to face him. "For the first time in ten years…I thought maybe I could love someone." Her eyes searched his. "But you said you weren't interested in that sort of thing back at the hay field when I asked you."

He retreated a step and let go of her arm, running over the conversation in his head and suddenly understanding. "I had a fiancée who said it was either my job or her. My job didn't have enough status or income for her. Doing these expeditions is like breathing to me. That's what I was thinking about when you asked me if I would ever get married and have kids. I just kind of let go of the idea after Emma dumped me."

Clarissa's voice softened. "Oh, I thought that dismissal was directed toward me."

He shook his head, finally comprehending what she was getting at. "You mean…you saw us…maybe sometime in the future?"

She turned her back again. "Now I'm embarrassed that I said anything. It doesn't matter."

The hurt and anger he felt over what Emma had done to him was still very raw. He'd closed that door, not wanting to open himself up to the possibility of that kind of pain ever again.

A gentle knock sounded. Naomi came in with two plates piled high with breakfast food on a tray. "Here you two are." She set the tray on the desk. "Take as much time as you need." She pulled out a small pink children's backpack she had tucked under her arm. "I noticed that pack you are carrying is torn to pieces. I thought you might want a replacement."

Clarissa stepped across the room and grasped her hands. "Thank you."

"You were always very special to me. I prayed for you every day and wondered what happened to you after you left here so suddenly." Naomi moved over to her desk and grabbed a photo from a pile. "Other people have wondered about you, too. Do you remember Sarah and Rochelle? The three of you were so close."

Clarissa looked at the photograph, and her eyes glazed with tears. "Of course I remember them."

"I'm planning a reunion for the girls who were here over that Christmas ten years ago. I hope you'll come."

Clarissa pressed the photo to her chest. "I'd like to."

Her voice had such longing in it. Was she thinking about how much they had to overcome to do something as normal as go to a reunion?

"Maybe I'll see you there, too, Ezra," Naomi said.

Clarissa interjected, "Oh, he's not my..." She shook her head.

After Naomi left, Clarissa handed him a plate of food. Hunger had been gnawing at his stomach for hours. He shoveled one forkful after another of scrambled eggs into his mouth.

As he ate, he picked up on Clarissa's nervous glances in his direction. He wasn't sure how to respond to what she'd said. She liked him and it seemed that she wished there could be more between them.

But would her feelings last when they were no longer forced together by circumstances? Was her attraction born out of a need for someone to cling to because they'd been in such a desperate situation? Or was there something deeper between them? He scraped his fork across the nearly empty plate and cleared his throat. He couldn't answer that question with any clarity, and he sure didn't want to feel the kind of pain Emma had caused him ever again. "I think I'll call my partner first, find out if the others made it off the mountain."

Clarissa gathered up the dishes and placed them back on the tray. "Yes, that's been bothering me, too."

He could hear the tension in her voice. The implications of what she had said lay between them, unresolved.

"And then it might take me a couple of tries to remember Officer Pitman's number. I wish I had my phone with me. The number is in my contacts list. I haven't memorized it," Ezra said.

He walked over to the desk and picked up the phone while Clarissa sat on the couch, looking at him in earnest. He took in a deep breath and dialed the number.

Clarissa could feel the heat rise up in her cheeks when Ezra looked directly at her. She was embarrassed by what she'd said. Of course someone like Ezra wouldn't be interested in someone like her.

Her stomach tied in knots as she listened to the phone ringing.

Ezra pulled the phone away from his ear. "What day is it?"

Clarissa drew a blank. She'd lost track of how much time had gone by while they were in the wilderness. Day had poured into night and night into day. They hadn't had a full night's sleep in days.

She shot to her feet and looked at the calendar Naomi had posted on her wall. "I think it must be Wednesday."

Ezra clicked the phone off. "Jack won't be reachable. He's out on another short expedition with a new group."

"If they made it back, we can call them directly. We can call Leonard or Jan," Clarissa said.

"I don't know their numbers off the top of my head. I need my phone."

"That would mean we'd have to go back to the office?"

"It's at my house," he said.

"Do you think Max would have figured out where you live, and assigned someone to watch that place, too?"

He rose to his feet and dropped his hands onto his hips. "It's no secret where I live. They could find out easily enough."

Clarissa's throat went tight with fear. There had to be another way besides going to a place that was so high risk. Ezra stood before her, the look on his face pensive. Why was he even trying to help her at this point?

"You don't have to do this, you know," she told him. "You got me back to town. This really is my problem. They're not after you unless you're with me."

"What kind of man would I be if I walked out of here and left you high and dry? We've seen this through this far. Let's finish it."

The weight of the gratitude she felt made her knees wobble. Even if he never wanted to see her again after all this was over, she admired him more than any man she'd ever known. He wasn't going to leave her when she needed him the most. "Thank you."

She shuffled through a stack of books until she retrieved a phone directory. "What if we called the police station directly and asked for the officer you trust? If he's there, he might be able to help us."

Ezra flipped through the phone book. "It's worth a try." He found the non-emergency number for the police and dialed it. A crisp sounding voice came across the line.

"Hello, can I please speak to Officer Pitman?" Ezra asked. A moment later he gave

Clarissa a thumbs-up, indicating that his friend was at the station.

She relaxed a little, enough to grab her beat-up backpack and start transferring things into the new pink backpack Naomi had given her.

"Hey, Grant, I'm here with a woman named Clarissa Jones…."

She listened as Ezra explained what had happened, and then gave one-and two-word responses to what the officer was saying. His expression grew grimmer. He cast a wary glance toward Clarissa and then he turned his back and lowered his voice.

Perspiration formed on Clarissa's forehead as she wrung her hands together. What had Max told the police?

Finally, Ezra hung up the phone. He continued to stare out the window.

"Ezra, what did he say?"

He turned to face her. "You were right. Max did come into town claiming that you stole from him and that you jumped bail. The police department has orders to pick you up if they see you. One of Max's henchmen must have posed as a bounty hunter. If the police caught you, you would have been turned over to him."

"None of it is true. I didn't steal from Max."

"I know that, but we have to be able to prove it," he said.

"Did he know anything about Leonard or the others?"

"There have been no reports—either of them coming out of the woods or of people being found dead. They must have at least made it out of the lodge. Another group would have gone through there by now."

"That's a good sign, I guess. What do we do now?"

"We've got to go to the police with something solid, otherwise they would be obligated to turn you back over to the state of California."

"I didn't take anything from him. He took everything from me, and now he wants me dead and I don't know why." Frustration laced her voice.

Ezra grabbed her hands. "That's what we have to figure out. I need you to tell me everything."

"I'm not sure where to start."

"You said that there was something off about the bank deposits for house sales."

"There wasn't anything illegal about it, so far as I could tell. It was just that there would be a deposit for me to take to the bank, and then I'd get the paperwork for the sale of a property a week after that. It seemed backward to me. I didn't think anything of it at the time. Max juggles a lot of properties. He's not an organized person. He's a salesman. That's why he had an assistant. I just figured he was mixed up about which chunk of money belonged to which property."

Ezra shifted his weight. "So you didn't say anything to Max about how odd that was?"

She shook her head. "The one time I brought it up was when he said a deposit was for a piece of property that I knew was not our listing anymore. I drove by that house every day on my way to work. I saw the sign for a different Realtor in the yard and figured the home owner must have dropped us for somebody else."

"And what did Max say when you pointed that out to him?"

"He shrugged and said he'd have to look into it." She thought for a moment. "Shortly after that, he came on to me…that was a few days after Sondra was fired." Clarissa took the money Max's wife had given her out of the backpack and stared at it.

Ezra moved toward her and pointed at the money. "What if the reason the deposits didn't match the date of sale for the properties was because the money wasn't coming from the property sales?"

"You mean that Max was counterfeiting or laundering money?"

"It's possible."

"But his wife gave me this money and I don't think she was in on anything," Clarissa said.

"Maybe his wife didn't realize the money was dirty. Think carefully about the sequence of events. Max sent his henchmen to the airport to get you after you had the money, right? Up to that point, his actions kind of implied he was trying to run you out of town rather than kill you."

"But Max thought I knew more than I did when I brought up the thing about the deposits and the properties. Or he was afraid I'd figure it out. That's when he came on to me. Maybe he thought he could get me on his side." Clarissa took in a breath as a realization came to her. "What if Max suspected Sondra was snooping in his office? Or that she saw something, but he wasn't sure, so he fired her?"

"Max saw you two talking a lot, right? He might have thought you were working together or that your loyalty would be to Sondra because you were close. Then when you had that money, he concluded you had it figured out. And if the money really is counterfeit, then you could use it as hard evidence against him. That was when he switched strategies from discrediting you to taking you out entirely."

Ezra paced. "I know one thing. This is not a local police problem. We need to talk to the

FBI." He flipped through the phone book. "We'll need a car to get to their offices. I don't think this is a conversation that should take place over the phone."

"Naomi might have something we can borrow."

Ten minutes later, they were headed across town. The FBI office was in a nondescript building that also housed offices for a chiropractor and a water quality inspector.

They took the elevator up to the third floor. Anxiety plagued Clarissa. What if Max had gotten to these guys, too? They stepped out into a carpeted hallway. Ezra found the right door and knocked. He offered her an encouraging smile and squeezed her hand. "This is going to work."

"I hope so."

A woman with short red hair, wearing a white shirt and navy skirt, opened the door.

"We need to talk to an FBI agent," Ezra said.

"I'm Agent Lewis." She stepped aside so they could enter the office. A second male agent sat behind a desk staring at a computer. "That's Agent Mayer."

"We think we may have evidence of a money laundering or counterfeiting operation taking place."

"Why don't you two take a seat and tell me what you know," said Agent Lewis.

Clarissa and Ezra settled in the hard plastic chairs while Agent Lewis sat in front of her laptop. She clicked through a few commands and kept her fingers on the keyboard.

Clarissa took the money out of the pink backpack. "This is Ezra Jefferson and my name is Clarissa Jones."

The agent jerked her fingers off the keyboard. Her face blanched, and she shot a glance toward Agent Mayer, who pushed his chair away from the desk. "Please excuse me for a moment while I make a call." She picked up her phone and stepped into an adjoining room. The male agent got up and left the room, as well.

Clarissa watched the clock as ten minutes passed. She could hear the muffled tones of the agent talking on the phone in the next room. Clarissa gripped the pink backpack. "I don't think we should stay here. Did you see the look on her face when I said our names? I think Max got to them, too."

Ezra rose to his feet. "You might be right."

They slipped through the office and down the hallway to stand by the elevator. She watched the numbers click by.

Agent Lewis came out of her office just as the elevator doors opened. "Hey." She ran toward them.

Ezra pulled Clarissa into the elevator. Reaching the ground floor, they raced across the lobby and out into the parking lot. Ezra searched for the car keys. Another car pulled into the lot, but not into a parking space.

"Ezra, hurry." Clarissa's heart raced.

The driver's door on the other car opened. Ezra found the keys and unlocked their car. As Clarissa pulled open her door, a voice shouted her name. She looked up, not immediately recognizing the person in front of her.

"I thought you were dead," Clarissa whispered.

Sondra walked toward her. "Clarissa." Her face was bright and welcoming.

Clarissa shook her head in disbelief. "But I saw the newspaper."

"We planted the story," Sondra said.

Clarissa took a step back, still shaking her head. "I don't understand."

"Clarissa, I'm an FBI agent. Max saw me when I came into town to pick you up. I managed to shake his henchmen off, and then we faked the story so he wouldn't try to pursue me. When the other agents went to find you, you had vanished off the face of the earth."

"So you know that Max was doing something illegal with money," Clarissa said.

"When the housing market went south, we suspected that he took to laundering money for the mob. I was looking for evidence that day in his office, but I didn't find anything. Though he couldn't prove anything, Max was suspicious and paranoid, so he got rid of me."

"I thought you were dead." Anger and joy wrestled within Clarissa. She'd thought she'd lost her friend.

Sondra pulled her into a hug. "I'm so sorry."

Agent Lewis ran out into the parking lot. "Clarissa, I was only calling Sondra. I wanted time to prepare you for the shock before she showed up. That's why I went into the other room."

Ezra came and stood by Clarissa. "She's been through a lot."

Agent Lewis touched Clarissa's elbow. "We do need to talk to you. Would you come back upstairs?"

She planted her feet and squared her shoulders. "Is this about catching Max?"

Agent Lewis nodded. "We would like to take a moment to find out what you and Mr. Jefferson know."

They returned to the office. Clarissa was led into a second room, occupied by a table and chair.

"I need to go get my laptop and call my supervisor." Agent Lewis went to do so.

Sondra came in and leaned against the door

frame. "I'm sorry I couldn't tell you when we were working together," she said. "I had no idea Max would go after you. The mob must have got word that he was under investigation, so he suspected everyone."

Clarissa stood up and offered her friend a sideways hug. "I'm glad you're okay. This is just a lot to process."

Agent Lewis came back into the room and set her laptop on the table. "Clarissa, I'm going to need to ask you a few questions."

Sondra left the office, closing the door behind her.

Agent Lewis placed her fingers on the keyboard. "Can you tell me when you first suspected Max of laundering money?"

"I didn't put it all together until a couple hours ago. Ezra helped me figure it out."

"Why were we unable to find you for the past few days?"

"Max's men started coming after me as soon as I arrived in Discovery. I feared for my life, and I needed to hide somewhere they wouldn't find me. Ezra runs a survival training program, and I talked him into taking me on one of his wilderness expeditions. Max found me anyway. I put a bunch of people's lives in danger—the others on the expedition. Ezra stayed with me to protect me, which meant they were left on their own. I still don't know if they are okay or not."

Agent Lewis placed her hand over Clarissa's. "We can find that out for you." She continued to ask questions about what had transpired in the weeks leading up to Clarissa fleeing California, and then for details about what had happened in the forest. "Can any of what happened to you when you were out in the wilderness be linked directly to Max?" she asked at last.

"Don is an employee of Max's. I didn't know the other men. I did see Max get out of the helicopter when those men came after us at the lodge."

Agent Lewis paused for a moment, tapping her pen on the desk. "Do you think the reason Max made advances toward you was because he thought maybe he could make you a coconspirator?"

"At the time I didn't think that, but now, with everything that I know, maybe he thought if I was involved with him, I wouldn't turn him in."

"We don't have a lot to nail Max with other than your word against his. I'm wondering if you would be willing to try to trap him into admitting to the laundering," said Agent Lewis.

"How would I do that?"

"Give him a call. Tell him you are tired of running and that you want to make a deal with him."

Fear shot through Clarissa like a bullet. "So I'd sit down face-to-face with Max," she said.

"It would be a public place. We'd have agents outside the restaurant and inside."

The thought of meeting her old boss terrified her, but she fought past it. "If it's the only way…I sure don't want him to get away with all this."

"Good. Then we'll make the phone call and set something up for later this afternoon."

This had to be done. As Agent Lewis retrieved a phone for her to make the call, Clarissa wished Ezra was sitting beside her instead of being questioned in the next room.

Ezra studied the tall woman sitting on the opposite side of the desk. Agent Mayer had stepped out, saying something about food.

Ezra narrowed his eyes at Sondra. "So you're Clarissa's friend?"

"Yes. And in case you are wondering, I truly am her friend. I didn't pretend to be her friend so I could get information out of her, if that's what you wanted to know."

"No, I…" Ezra shook his head, but then said, "Yeah, I guess that's what I was asking."

"Clarissa is probably glad that you're looking out for her."

"Clarissa can look out for herself," Ezra said.

"I know that. She's a very capable woman. But you still feel kind of protective of her, don't you?" Sondra shifted in her office chair.

"Is that one of the questions you're supposed to be asking me?"

"As an agent, no. As Clarissa's friend, yes."

"Maybe you should stick to the official questions." He pointed to her laptop.

"But you do care for her?"

Ezra stared at his hands. "Yes, I do. I just don't know what that means to me right now."

"If you're not sure, don't mess with her head. She's had a lot of people walk out on her in her life, and she deserves to have someone who will stay," Sondra said.

"I don't know if I can be that guy for her."

Sondra studied him for a moment. "At least you're honest. Okay, on to the official questions. Can you tell me what you know about Max Fitzgerald? What level of interaction have you had with him, and what Clarissa has told you?"

Ezra recounted everything he had witnessed and what Clarissa had told him. After about ten minutes of questioning, the door to the other room opened. Agent Lewis stepped out with Clarissa behind her. Clarissa's expression was solemn, and her skin had lost much of its color.

Ezra rose to his feet as she locked on to him with her eyes. "What's going on?" he asked.

Agent Lewis rested a hand on her shoulder. "Clarissa has agreed to wear a wire and to meet with Max to try to get him to admit to his illegal activities."

Ezra felt as though he'd been punched in the stomach. "You want her to sit down face-to-face with that man?"

"Ezra, it's the only way they can make a solid case against him." Clarissa tucked a strand of hair behind her ear. Her eyes held a pleading look. "I've already made the phone call. Max has agreed to meet me in four hours, and he's promised to come alone."

"I don't know if that is such a good idea." Max's men had been relentless. Why would they simply back off now?

"Mr. Jefferson, you are free to go," said Agent Lewis.

A kind of panic that he'd never felt before rose up in him. "I want to be there with her."

"I'm afraid we can't allow that and risk Max walking away. She agreed to come alone, as well. She needs to appear completely vulnerable."

"Appear? You mean you'll be close by?"

"Agent Mayer will be in the restaurant, and Sondra and I will be listening in the van."

"I guess you have it all worked out then." Ezra couldn't stop the encroaching helplessness.

"Like I said, Mr. Jefferson—you are free to go. There's no indication that Mr. Fitzgerald will come after you unless you are with Miss Jones."

Sondra cleared her throat. "Maybe Ezra would like to have a moment alone to say good-bye to Clarissa."

He nodded. "Please."

Sondra tugged on Agent Lewis's sleeve. "We'll be out in the hall."

As soon as the door shut behind them, Ezra turned to face Clarissa. "I don't suppose there is any way I can talk you out of this?"

"I want to make sure I do everything to guarantee that Max goes to jail. It has to be done." Ezra saw the resolve in her eyes…and the fear.

He rested a hand on her shoulder. She closed her eyes.

"I wish there was some other way—a way where I could be there for you through this."

"It's not your fight, Ezra. It never was. You've done more for me than any man should have to do. You kept your word—you said you would get me out of that wilderness alive and you did."

She was letting him off the hook, but he didn't want to go. "I feel like I'm throwing you to the wolves. I can't walk away."

"They don't want you around." She glanced at the floor, then lifted her head and locked him in her gaze. "I don't understand why you're still here. They said you were free to go."

He didn't understand it himself. Why couldn't he let go? She was in the hands of the professionals now. "Guess I want to see this thing to the end. To know that Max can't hurt you or anybody else."

She nodded. Her gaze delved beneath his skin. "Is that what it is?" A lilt in her voice hinted at some emotion she was trying to hide.

The door swung open, and Sondra poked her head in. "I don't mean to rush you, but we have a lot of setup to do, and Clarissa will need some prep, as well."

Ezra offered a faint smile. "I understand. Be safe, Clarissa." With one more backward glance, he opened the door and headed down the stairs.

The long walk across town gave him time to think, but his thoughts remained a jumbled mess. He felt adrift, at loose ends. It was as if he didn't know what to do with himself now that responsibility for Clarissa's safety had been taken off his shoulders. He stopped in at the Black Bear Inn to see if Leonard or the others had checked back in.

The clerk shook his head. "No one has come by, and their suitcases are still in storage."

Ezra felt a heaviness as he crossed the street to Jefferson Expeditions. Today would have been the day the group got back if things had gone as planned. He stepped into his office and called search and rescue to advise them of the situation. If the helicopters couldn't find the group, he'd have to go up himself later today. Search and rescue promised him some men and dogs if needed.

Next, he looked around the office to see if it was still secure. Nothing indicated that Max's men had broken in. His business website would have provided enough information for them to know the general area where to look for Clarissa once they'd concluded she'd gone on the expedition.

He locked the place up, got in his car and drove home to his cabin outside of town along the river. He showered and ate with the words of the FBI agent echoing in his head: *you are free to go*. He stood on the porch listening to the rushing water. He was struck by how what he used to describe as peaceful now felt lonely. In that moment, he knew he couldn't let Clarissa face this confrontation alone, regardless of what the professionals thought.

Clarissa brought the car she'd borrowed from the agents to the curb. She laced her fingers together to try to stop the trembling. The recording device she wore pressed against her rib cage.

The restaurant where Max waited was just around the corner.

She took in a deep breath.

Agent Mayer was already in the restaurant. Agent Lewis and Sondra were in a van across the street.

Clarissa pushed the car door open and stepped out onto the curb. She rounded the corner.

Her legs felt as limp as cooked noodles as she made her way up the sidewalk. A group of people entered the restaurant a block and a half away. She stepped deliberately as her heart pounded against her rib cage. This had to be done, but having to sit across from Max and look him in the eye terrified her more than all she and Ezra had been through in the mountains. His charismatic salesman personality had camouflaged the monster beneath his skin for years, but now she knew he was pure evil.

She hadn't ever been good at reading people's character, especially where men were concerned. Except for Ezra. He had proved himself. It stung that he wasn't romantically interested in someone like her. But Clarissa would admire him for rest of her life. She stopped ten feet from the door of the restaurant and steeled herself for what she needed to do.

A car door opened behind her. She turned her head just as a man reached out for her and dragged her into the backseat of the car, which immediately pulled away from the curb and sped up the street. Clarissa barely had time to absorb what had happened before the man in the front passenger seat turned around and sneered at her. It was Max Fitzgerald.

"Did you really think I'd fall for that scam?" Max looked at the man who had yanked her into the car. "Get the wire off her."

She looked at the man next to her. It was Don. "Where is it?" he demanded. She saw murder in his eyes. He pulled her shirt to one side and ripped the tiny microphone off, rolled down the window and threw it out.

"Head out of town, someplace secluded," Max said to the driver. "This has to happen with no possibility of witnesses—and in a place where no one will find the body."

"Does it look like we have any kind of a tail?" the driver asked, keeping his eyes on the road. She recognized the driver as the square-jawed thug who had attacked her in the forest.

Don chuckled. "Doesn't look like they got their act together fast enough."

His words were like knife blades through her skin.

So Max would win, after all.

Ezra watched as Clarissa was grabbed and yanked into a car, just as he was about to pull into a parking space. With his heart in his throat, he eased onto the street so as not to call attention to himself as he followed the fleeing car. He gripped the steering wheel. It took every ounce of self-control not to speed.

The car was moving too fast and was already too far ahead for him to stop it by causing an accident. He couldn't risk injuring Clarissa in any case. Max's car took a left turn. Clearly, they were headed out of town toward the highway.

The agents must have seen and heard some of the scuffle when Clarissa was taken, but they would be delayed in their pursuit by the need to get the van turned around. They might even have lost sight of Max's car. He didn't know the agents' phone numbers so he dialed 911 and alerted them to the situation. When he caught up with these guys, he might need help.

He turned up a side street so as not to clue Max in that he was following them. He knew all the shortcuts through town. They wouldn't see his car until they were on the highway, and then they would probably assume he was just another anonymous driver headed in the same direction.

Even as he said a quick prayer for Clarissa's safety, doubt invaded his thoughts. He knew in the moment that he watched her disappear into the car that the agents had been wrong about him. He wasn't free to go. What he and Clarissa had been through together bound them to each other. More than that, he knew why the home that he loved had felt so empty. Without Clarissa, everything would be that way from now on. He loved her.

As he pulled out onto the highway, he only hoped the realization hadn't come too late.

Clarissa winced as Don dug his fingers into her forearm. Her heartbeat drummed in her ear. The yellow lines of the highway clipped by.

"Got to be a place to turn off here somewhere, right?" said the driver.

"Like I know this part of the country," Don said.

"There." Max pointed to a sign that said Spanish Creek 2 Miles. "That's got to be some sort of out-of-the-way hiking trail or river."

The driver slowed the car and hit the turn signal. Right before he turned, a blue Jeep passed him on the left.

"Jerk," said the driver.

They turned onto a dirt road. "How far?"

"We need to get back here quite a ways. I don't want any chance that some do-gooder hiker stumbles on us," said Max.

Don chuckled as his grip cut off the circulation in her arm.

So this was it. She was going to die alone. Clarissa regretted not telling Ezra more directly that she loved him.

Ezra zoomed his Jeep past Max's car when it became clear they were turning. He pulled over to the shoulder, and the back tires spat out gravel as he turned around without stopping. Spanish Creek Road forked about three miles into the forest. While it was important that he avoid detection, he needed to stay close enough to know which way they went. Otherwise, he could lose them, and any chance of getting Clarissa out of the forest alive.

He phoned in to the police station again to alert them to where he was headed.

He turned onto the dirt road and slowed down. No sign of Max's car. He sped up, searching for any sign of the other car. He drove until he came to where the road split. He turned onto the fork that led north, driving for several minutes. Seeing no sign of the other car, he headed back toward the other fork. The second road straightened out for about a half-mile stretch. He breathed a sigh of relief when a dust cloud in the distance told him he had made the right choice. He slowed down, waiting for the car to disappear around a corner.

There had been at least two men in the car, the one driving and the one who had gotten into the backseat with Clarissa. If he sped up and rammed the car to disable it, he risked not being able to overpower them before he could get to Clarissa—or worse, injuring her in the crash. The better strategy was to surprise them once they'd stopped. He hung back, watching an uphill section of the road until the car came into view. He waited until it took another turn, onto a road he knew dead-ended. He drove as fast as he dared on the gravel road until he was about forty yards from the end.

Ezra parked his car and sprinted toward a high spot that would provide a perfect view of the place where the men had gone. He pushed himself to run faster, praying that there would be some buildup before they killed Clarissa, giving him time to intervene. He got to the top of the rock formation and peered down. The two men were digging a grave, while Max kept an eye on Clarissa. Her hands were tied, but not her feet. Only one of the men had a gun visible on his belt. Ezra couldn't tell if Max had a gun because he wore a jacket.

All of this was good. Ezra moved stealthily down the rocks toward the trees that surrounded where the men were digging. Using the woods for cover, Ezra worked his way toward Max and Clarissa. The diggers were a good thirty yards away. Max was a big man, but not muscular.

Ezra waited until the guy with the gun wandered away before making his move. He pounced on Max, disabling him with a single blow to the chest. Max groaned in pain and crumpled to the ground.

Ezra reached for Clarissa just as a hand grabbed the back of his shirt. He was glad to see it wasn't the thug with the gun. The henchman yanked Ezra back and landed a clumsy blow to the side of his head. Ezra whirled around and hit him hard three times in the head, throat, stomach.

The second thug emerged from the trees. He'd taken his gun holster off while digging the hole and had dropped it on the ground. Ezra leaped for the gun and held it on the man, who backed up with his hands in the air.

When he whirled around, he saw that Max had recovered and was leading Clarissa back to the car. He pushed her through the driver's-side door and then got in himself. Ezra darted toward them, trying to get close enough for an effective pistol shot. He aimed for a tire just as Max turned the car around. As the car lumbered forward on the washboard road, Ezra ran after it and shot at the tires again. The car continued to move but never gained speed as the tires slowly deflated.

Arms pumping, Ezra raced to catch up. When he glanced over his shoulder, one of the thugs was getting to his feet, but swaying.

Max got out of the car, ran to the passenger side and yanked Clarissa out. He had a gun in his hand, which he must have retrieved from the car. Max shoved Clarissa into a grove of aspen trees.

Had Max been pushed to the point of desperation where he would kill Clarissa even if there was a witness? Ezra doubted it. The new plan was probably to kill him, too. He entered the aspen grove. The white-and-black bark of the thin, close-together trees created a sort of labyrinth that was hard to see through. He caught a flash of color and moved toward it, aware that Max's plan might be to lure him to a vulnerable spot and then shoot him.

Ezra's heart drummed in his ears as he slipped around the trees. He pushed aside mental pictures of Clarissa being killed. He was no good to her if he let that fear take over. He stopped and pushed his back against a tree. Enough dry leaves littered the ground that he should hear the crunch of footsteps if Clarissa and Max were still moving. Wind gusted around him. Aspen leaves clacked and chattered on the branches, but he couldn't detect anything that sounded human.

He wove deeper into the forest, pushing down the rising anxiety. He would find Clarissa. She would get out of this alive. He said a prayer as he took in a breath and worked his way to the edge of the grove.

He stepped out into an open meadow, still seeing no sign of Max. He turned in a half circle, scanning the area around him.

"Ezra!" Clarissa shouted his name.

He whirled around. Max had stepped out of the trees and was aiming at him, some thirty feet away. But when Clarissa shouted, he turned the gun back toward the woods.

Ezra was too far away to make a shot that counted, and now Max was going to shoot Clarissa for warning him. As he ran, the world seemed to move in slow motion. He saw Max raise the gun and step toward the trees. He heard Clarissa's muffled scream.

The shot from Max's gun pummeled Ezra's ears as he raised his gun and aimed for Max's knee. Max groaned in agony and crumpled to the ground. Ezra raced past him into the trees.

Dark red blood stained the white bark of an aspen. The images of his life without Clarissa floated free and rose to the surface. He'd been too late in saying he loved her. And now he would never get the chance.

"Clarissa!" Agony and regret colored each syllable he uttered. He said her name again more softly. Blinded by sorrow, he pushed through the trees, but didn't see her anywhere. He followed the dotted trail of blood.

He found her lying on her side as blood spread across her shoulder. She shuddered with pain, unable to speak. He cut her free of the rope that bound her hands behind her back and lifted her into his arms.

Her words came in quick, pain-filled gasps. "I ran…hid in the trees. He got me…anyway."

"Just stay with me." He touched his hand to her cheek as he gritted his teeth. "It's going to be okay. We'll get you to the hospital."

"I… Oh, Ezra. I thought I wasn't going to see you again." She closed her eyes.

"Hang on for me, Clarissa. I can fix this." He wasn't sure if he was telling the truth about that. Even though Max wasn't going anywhere, at least one thug was still stalking around the woods, and Ezra's car was a long ways away.

As he headed back, Clarissa in his arms, he could hear Max's cries for help. Even if the thug could help Max they wouldn't get far on two shredded tires. But Ezra and Clarissa wouldn't be safe until they'd put some distance between themselves and their attackers.

He stepped free of the trees and walked up the road, increasing his pace. Clarissa was light as a bird in his arms. He walked faster. His Jeep came into view, and he loaded her carefully inside. Her eyes were still closed.

"Clarissa, are you still with me?" She opened her eyes and nodded. "You have to stay with me, okay?"

He jumped into the driver's seat and pushed the accelerator to the floor. The back of the car fishtailed as he sped up the road. Within minutes, he pulled out onto the highway. He still saw no sign of the police. He yanked his phone out and informed them about Max and the thugs.

Ezra raced into the parking lot of the hospital, braking so suddenly that the wheels squealed. He jumped out of the car. When he lifted Clarissa out of her seat, he saw that the bloody spot on her shoulder had grown.

He burst into the E.R. Within moments the staff surrounded him, taking Clarissa from his arms. He stood for a long moment staring at the blood on his shirt.

"Sir." A woman's voice broke through his numbness. "Why don't you take a seat? We'll come and get you as soon as we have her stabilized."

He collapsed into a waiting room chair and stared at the ceiling until it blurred.

His arms felt empty.

Clarissa had a vague sensation of swimming to the surface in a very deep lake. She opened her eyes and saw only bright lights before she was plunged beneath the water again. The faint memory of being carried by Ezra tickled the corners of her awareness.

"Clarissa?" A featherlight touch brushed her forearm. It took some effort for her to open her eyes.

Gradually, Ezra's face came into focus—his soft smile and wide brown eyes.

She opened her mouth to speak, but no words came out.

"Don't push yourself. The bullet was quite a shock to your body. You lost a lot of blood. It tore up your shoulder muscle pretty good, but missed anything major."

The dulcet bass tones of his voice warmed her heart. She closed her eyes as the events that led to her being in this hospital bed came back in a flash of violent memory. She shuddered. "Max?"

"In jail, along with his little helpers. It's going to take quite a while for the lawyers to put together the list of charges against him, in both California and Montana."

A nurse entered the room holding a tray of food. "I was hoping you would be awake." She placed the tray on the table. "I know you're still weak. But it would speed your recovery if you could get some nourishment in you." She looked over at Ezra. "And I believe this young man is willing to help make that happen."

Ezra smiled. "We'll give it a try." His fingers continued to trace a pattern on Clarissa's arm. After the nurse left, he turned to face her. "Are you thirsty?"

Her throat was parched. She nodded and reached out for the plastic cup with the cover and straw. Her hand shook. Ezra steadied it by wrapping his hand around hers and helping her get it to her mouth. She sipped. The cool liquid felt wonderful going down her throat.

"I was pretty thirsty. How long have I been asleep?"

"About twelve hours." He handed her a container of Jell-O and a spoon. She tried to pull the foil cover off and frowned when she couldn't get it open.

"I'm really weak."

He gently took the Jell-O from her hands. "Let me help you with that." He peeled away the cover and then, holding her hand steady, placed the container back in it.

She ate a few bites before putting it back on the tray. Maybe it was just the trauma of all she had been through, or the painkillers, but something between her and Ezra had shifted. He seemed more…attentive. He looked at her, and her face grew warm. She cleared her throat and reached for the toast on her tray.

"If you're up to it, I have a surprise for you."

"A surprise?" Her mind reeled with the possibilities. When she looked into his eyes, she saw a deeper affection than she had seen before. Was the surprise about…them?

"Why don't you get some sleep? I'll be back in about forty-five minutes."

She nodded. He turned the light out and disappeared down the hallway. It took her only minutes to drift off into a deep sleep. She awoke when she sensed that someone had stepped into the room. She saw the silhouette of a man in the darkness.

The fleeting thought that one of Max's men had come to finish her off paralyzed her with fear.

And then she heard the soft tones of Ezra's voice. "Are you awake?"

"You scared me half to death."

"Sorry, I thought switching on the light would be too harsh if you were still asleep," he said. "Can I turn it on now?"

She covered her eyes. "Sure."

Seeing his bright face washed away the final residue of fear over all that she had been through.

"So are you ready for your surprise?" He stepped closer to the hospital bed and rested his hand on her good shoulder.

"Yes, I'm ready."

"Okay, guys, you can come in," Ezra said.

One by one, Leonard, Jan, Ken and Bruce stepped through the door. Joy leaped through Clarissa to see her friends safe and sound.

"I can't believe it. When did you get into town? What happened?"

Jan ran over to her and gave her a careful hug. "I'm so glad to see your sweet face."

Leonard stepped forward and gripped the rail. "Good to see you, kid."

Bruce moved close, as well. "After you two diverted attention to yourselves, the rest of us went and hid in the woods, thinking we'd go back and radio for help once those men had left."

Leonard ran his hands through his salt-and-pepper hair. "Unfortunately, they left a man there to be the lookout."

Ken joined the others at her bedside. "So we decided to hike back out the way we'd come."

"I think we made pretty good time," said Bruce.

"We caught most of our food on the way down," Ken said, beaming with pride.

"Best survival school ever," added Bruce.

"Anyway—" Jan patted Clarissa's hand "—when we got to the base of the mountain, the van had been disabled, so we had to hike into town.

"And that's the story of how we got here," said Leonard.

Clarissa shook her head in disbelief. The four of them had truly become a team, even in telling what had happened to them.

"That's pretty amazing," she said.

"*You're* pretty amazing," said Jan. "Ezra told us what the two of you went through. I'm so grateful you're okay, honey."

Clarissa couldn't contain her happiness. "I feel like God has given me the family I never had. I'll never forget you guys."

"You won't be able to forget us." Leonard turned and looked at the others. "I say we make the survival school an annual event, a reunion of sorts."

They all nodded in agreement.

Jan squeezed Ezra's arm. "We'll leave you two alone."

"We'll come back tomorrow when you're feeling stronger, kid," Leonard said as he left the room.

Bruce, Jan and Ken all shuffled out after him.

The door closed behind them. Ezra pulled a chair close to Clarissa's bed. "They are something, those four, aren't they?"

"Lesser people would have been angry with me about everything that happened," Clarissa said.

"They're good people. They're just happy that you're out of danger. And speaking of which, Sondra and that other agent are going to want to talk to you tomorrow if you are up to it."

"I figured that," she said. She turned slightly to one side in the hospital bed. There was a heaviness in the room, as though there was something more that needed to be said. She stared at the ceiling. "Thank you, Ezra, for everything. For saving my life."

"You saved me a couple of times, too, you know." His chair scraped across the floor. He rested his arm on the railing. His head was very close to hers. Wide brown eyes studied her. He reached up and brushed a wisp of hair off her forehead.

The look in his eyes contained an intensity she hadn't seen before.

The intimacy of the moment made her nervous enough to start babbling. "So I guess you go back to your job and…I'm not sure what happens to me…where I'm going to go or anything," she said.

He continued to stroke her forehead. "How about you stay here in Discovery?"

"I…I've always liked it here."

"I'd like it if you stayed. I'd like to get to know you better, under not so trying circumstances."

Warmth spread through her midsection all the way down to her toes. "I think I'd like that, too, Ezra."

"Maybe I can do something really ordinary and boring, like take you out to dinner."

"I'd like that."

He stood up, leaned over and kissed her full on the mouth. She opened her eyes when he pulled free of the kiss.

"I sure don't want you ever leaving again." He looked at the floor and then back up at her. "When I thought I might lose you out there in the forest, and when you were shot, I realized… I saw my life without you, and I knew that I loved you."

Her eyes warmed with tears. She reached up and touched his cheek. "Oh, Ezra, I love you, too. Ordinary and boring sound wonderful to me."

He touched her cheek with a single finger. "I'm looking forward to it."

As she stared into his deep brown eyes, she realized that not only had God given her the family she'd never had, but also a man whose love would be as deep as the ocean.

* * * * *

Dear Reader,

Even though Clarissa and I have very different backgrounds, we both have had to learn to ask for help and to trust that it will be there even if past experience tells us otherwise. Clarissa believes that she must solve all her problems alone because no one was ever there for her in her childhood to help her. Her flight through the wilderness is also a journey in which she discovers that there are kind and good people everywhere. People who want to help and are willing to forgive.

As a child, I got the message that I was on my own to work through problems and emotions, largely because of the chaos created by an alcoholic father. One of the hardest things I have had to learn to do was ask for help, whether it's with a task or working through troubling emotions. People never cease to amaze me. God has brought many generous people into my life, even some who intuitively know when I need help. We don't need to be defined by our childhood and there is always a chance for healing and redemption.

Sharon Dunn

Questions for Discussion

1. Why does Clarissa have a hard time believing anyone would help her with her problems?

2. Why did she put all her energy into her job working for Max?

3. What events led to Clarissa choosing to become a Christian? Who influenced her in that decision?

4. Much like Joseph in the Bible, Clarissa tries to do the right thing by telling Stella Fitzgerald what kind of man Max really is. For doing the right thing, she loses everything. Have you ever had a Joseph situation in your life?

5. What was the most exciting scene for you?

6. Who was your favorite character? Why?

7. What do Ezra and the other members of the expedition do that helps Clarissa learn to trust?

8. Have you ever known someone like Clarissa? In what way?

9. What sort of survival skills did Ezra teach the members of the group?

10. Did you agree with the decisions that Ezra made as a leader? What were some of those hard choices?

11. A huge part of survival in a wilderness situation is mental, keeping your head in the right place. How did Ezra do that? How does he teach Clarissa to do that?

12. How does Clarissa get the family she never had?

13. Would you like to have a job like Ezra's or go on a survival expedition?

14. Why is Ezra afraid to commit to Clarissa even though he has feelings for her? What changes his mind?

15. What do you think is the overall theme of the book?

LARGER-PRINT BOOKS!

GET 2 FREE LARGER-PRINT NOVELS PLUS 2 FREE MYSTERY GIFTS

Love Inspired®

Larger-print novels are now available...

REQUEST YOUR FREE BOOKS!
2 FREE WHOLESOME ROMANCE NOVELS
IN LARGER PRINT
PLUS 2
FREE
MYSTERY GIFTS

HEARTWARMING™

Wholesome, tender romances

YES! Please send me 2 FREE Harlequin® Heartwarming Larger-Print novels and my 2 FREE mystery gifts (gifts worth about $10). After receiving them, if I don't wish to receive any more books, I can return the shipping statement marked "cancel." If I don't cancel, I will receive 4 brand-new larger-print novels every month and be billed just $4.99 per book in the U.S. or $5.74 per book in Canada. That's a savings of at least 23% off the cover price. It's quite a bargain! Shipping and handling is just 50¢ per book in the U.S. and 75¢ per book in Canada.* I understand that accepting the 2 free books and gifts places me under no obligation to buy anything. I can always return a shipment and cancel at any time. Even if I never buy another book, the two free books and gifts are mine to keep forever.

161/361 IDN F47N

Name _____ (PLEASE PRINT) _____

Address _____ Apt. # _____

City _____ State/Prov. _____ Zip/Postal Code _____

Signature (if under 18, a parent or guardian must sign) _____

Mail to the **Harlequin® Reader Service:**
IN U.S.A.: P.O. Box 1867, Buffalo, NY 14240-1867
IN CANADA: P.O. Box 609, Fort Erie, Ontario L2A 5X3

* Terms and prices subject to change without notice. Prices do not include applicable taxes. Sales tax applicable in N.Y. Canadian residents will be charged applicable taxes. Offer not valid in Quebec. This offer is limited to one order per household. Not valid for current subscribers to Harlequin Heartwarming larger-print books. All orders subject to credit approval. Credit or debit balances in a customer's account(s) may be offset by any other outstanding balance owed by or to the customer. Please allow 4 to 6 weeks for delivery. Offer available while quantities last.

Your Privacy—The Harlequin® Reader Service is committed to protecting your privacy. Our Privacy Policy is available online at www.ReaderService.com or upon request from the Harlequin Reader Service.

We make a portion of our mailing list available to reputable third parties that offer products we believe may interest you. If you prefer that we not exchange your name with third parties, or if you wish to clarify or modify your communication preferences, please visit us at www.ReaderService.com/consumerschoice or write to us at Harlequin Reader Service Preference Service, P.O. Box 9062, Buffalo, NY 14269. Include your complete name and address.

HWDIR13R